PRAISE FOR
MIRACLE ON SNOWBIRD LAKE

Miracle on Snowbird Lake is powerful and gripping. Stan Bednarz keeps you turning pages with his vivid portrayal of New York's frigid north country as he shines a bright light on the best and worst the human spirit has to offer. Bednarz is a talented new writer and his story is extremely compelling.

> Tim Green, NY Times bestselling author of numerous suspense novels including *Unstoppable*, *False Convictions*, and *Above the Law*

Miracle on Snowbird Lake grabbed me from beginning to end. Stan Bednarz's ability to paint a picture with words is truly a gift.

> Fran Fernandez, author of *The Best is Yet to Come*;
> Christian conference speaker

Stan Bednarz's mystery novel is intriguing, thought provoking, and emotionally moving—the kind of book impossible to put down after reading the first page.

> Ronald A. Hart, international author and screenwriter, England

Bednarz has created rich and deeply moving characters, especially in the pastor. The reader can't help but feel connected to them. We are made to see how one man can touch many lives and make a difference in the world. I was unable to keep away from it and just had to read on.

> Fausto Angelina, retired high school English teacher, Canada

Miracle on Snowbird Lake

Can Hope penetrate the darkest night?

Stan Bednarz

MIRACLE ON
SNOWBIRD LAKE

Deep River
B O O K S

Published by Carmichael Publishing, an imprint of Deep River Books
Sisters, Oregon
www.deepriverbooks.com

ISBN-13: 9781937756673
ISBN-10: 193775667X

Library of Congress: 2012952353

Cover design by David Litwin, Purefusion Media

Printed in the United States of America
2013—First Edition

10 9 8 7 6 5 4 3 2 1

This book is dedicated to my lovely wife, Mary.
You sacrificed moments when we could have deepened our relationship.
Your love and patience are what made this book possible in the first place.

Miracle on Snowbird Lake

Prologue

Eleven-year-old Annie Davis didn't mind that it was 1988 and the near death of summer. She had the beginning of middle school to care about when she glided off on her navy blue bike beneath a canopy of trees at the steps of her father's church.

Yellow leaves dipped in the sun and twirled in the wind, preparing for the dance of fall on dull blades of grass. Annie breathed in the sanctified air. Her backpack was full of fresh-cut paper and notebooks in the colors of a rainbow.

Her father met her on the concrete steps and hugged her like a lumberjack until her feet left the ground. As he set her down, stepping back, he admired her angelic glow. He loved her innocent smile and the way her auburn curls danced around her shoulders. His only daughter was transitioning into a teenager—but no matter her age, he could look into her eyes and find the child inside.

School just days away, he imagined her stepping into a place where boys would laugh at her unpretentious smile, dive into the wonder of her eyes as she delighted in everything from ashen stones to white-ribbed clouds. He thought a good father needed to step back, give her space, let her have room to grow beyond his grip.

Leaving the church steps, she rode her bike around the horseshoe park, passing the proudly erected steeples of the Protestant churches. As she passed the pearly white gazebo, she turned to smile at her father, a still frame that would scar his mind forever.

He could not have known that it would be his last glimpse of her cherub face.

Annie turned down Main Street, which should have led her home. She never made it. It was as if she disappeared into another time and place. In her father's mind, she stopped growing; she froze at eleven.

A few yards from the main road leading home, her bike was found upside down, face cards pinned to the spokes of the wheels, flapping in the breeze. Her backpack was never recovered, but a few scrunched papers tripped in the wind like ghostly tumbleweeds. The field could be seen from the Davis home, a torturous view of tall weeds, silent accomplices to an obvious abduction. Police and town volunteers searched the area of her disappearance into the night until white orbs of light crisscrossed the railroad tracks.

Dutch Hollow, once a safe bedroom community with more graves than living residents, locked down that night. When daylight came, the chain-linked swings in the park lay empty, and children no longer roamed free. A change was felt, as if a thick invisible current of air had dropped from the sky.

In the shadow of the Adirondack Mountains, the town rallied together for a while. They passed out flyers, held meetings, funded a $5000 reward, and set up a nondescript call center with a toll-free number for tips leading to the whereabouts of Annie Davis.

At Mimi's Diner, the patrons seemed lost, hardly noticing the yolk on their shirts or the coffee on their breath. One weathered customer leaned over his slippery red stool to pay for his breakfast. "Like finding an acorn among thickets. Endless branches slapping your face." His loose change clattered on the counter.

Donna Brushton listened to the old man, who seemed to be proud of his gloomy report. She was sitting alone in a booth nearby. She was new in town and had rented a flat above the diner. Pursing her lips, she sipped her black and bitter coffee. Then she turned and looked deep into the bosom of the mountains. For now, she kept her thoughts, held her tongue. The town wasn't ready for a psychic just yet.

One
The Death Dance

1989—One year and four months later

Annie's face was printed in black and white as if this made her less alive, less dimensional. Pastor Robert Davis held the flyers with an earnest grip in the windblown snow. When he closed his eyes against the lateral crystals that pricked his face like small needles, he could see her colors: auburn hair, copper skin, and a pearly smile—a smile that could fill a blank white canvas.

Coat flapping against the wind, fur-lined hat pulled snug, he broke through the hard snow toward the Big M grocery store. Strangers opened the door as they headed outside, and he wedged himself into the vestibule that felt like a penalty booth for a rogue hockey player.

As he lifted his head between the vacuum of cold and hot air, he couldn't find Annie's picture on the bulletin board. Her face was buried under fresh notices, as if a moving sale with cherrywood furniture or a lost-dog reward was more important than his daughter. After more than a year, they had run out of room for her face. He clenched the fingers of his black leather gloves with his teeth and tacked several more of her wet, limp posters around the periphery of the bulletin board. He felt his life on edge; what was left of his family, wife and son, teetered in the balance as he searched for Annie when no one else would.

A parade of boots had made mush behind his feet, and he muscled the tack in deep with his thumb.

Turning to leave, he forced the door open into the swirling snow. A young mother with her daughter tripped in the wind, attempting to enter the doorway. The reverend politely threw his body against the door, shielding their entry. The mother shouted through the wind, "Thank you, sir!"

She held her daughter in a strong grip. The wonder of the world was written in the little girl's face, never more alive, while she clung innocently to her mother's arm. Thick flakes melted down her reddened cheeks and clung to her blonde hair.

His eyelids stung, nostrils too, but he kept his eyes wide. How he wished he had never let Annie go when the winds of evil blew that day. But how does one predict when that wind will blow?

The warm waters of Lake Ontario had brewed up a first good storm for early December, and it broke across the plateau of farm fields, filling up the valley towns buffeted against the Adirondacks. Several sad, worn towns waited for him on his route home to Dutch Hollow.

As he climbed into his Oldsmobile, his heavy black box on wheels, he wished he had gotten studs on his tires.

His wipers attacked the snow like dull rubber swords, twin boys in a game of war. His defroster growled until it found a rhythmic whirr. He paused and listened to the wind seeking entrance underneath his car until it turned into a ghostly whistle invading the tendrils of his mind, rising above the heater's own cadence. He pressed his head on the steering wheel until he could feel the cold notch into his forehead. "Is this your idea, God, this frozen hell?"

Annie was no longer in the news. The public search had ended months ago. A few calls still trickled into the office of Tom Brower, the sheriff: paranoid mothers, drama addicts, and self-proclaimed psychics. News. Something had to happen bigger than the storm, like an avalanche of information cascading down to the sheriff's door.

Robert Davis envisioned that empty trailer in the back parking lot of the state police barracks. He imagined what it looked like now. Snow spitting against the door, windows covered in frost, boxes full of his daughter's information, old computers icy cold, and mice happily living underneath the scattered debris.

The sun's dim circle faded behind the flurries as if unable to burst through. He simply drove. No prayer to be offered, no parting of the white waves, just driving with death around every corner.

The Olds fishtailed down a hill. Snow-covered road signs were his only way to mark where it was safe to drive.

Route 26 was blanketed with snow as he headed toward Lowville, but he could see the serpentine Black River beside him, the current so swift that the snow melted as it fell into the moving water. In every season it defined the town beside it, a brutish landmark, unforgiving. Nothing held back its venomous bite.

Lights from other cars and a Mack truck appeared on the warped horizon, and that's when the death dance started, as the yellow lights penetrated his scant vision. He found himself in a game of chicken at random points on the highway. Roads without lines.

Just maybe this child thief is laughing in the snow, maybe this scum pod, this amoeba of a man somehow hides in the mountains and has made his bed on virgin snow without tracks for miles to find him; he stands there laughing, and even an echo only sends snow tripping down fir branches harmlessly on the white shadow.

Such were the thoughts that drove him to the edge of insanity. They haunted his dreams at night. They stole moments once devoted to prayer. This unknown stranger tugged at the core of his faith.

He had a beeper phone for emergencies, and it lit up, vibrated and hummed on his cold leather seat. He knew Mary had sent out her signal, a one-way sign of her thawing reservoir of love. It was certainly not safe for him to be alone, his mind having been carved by a devil's knife.

Her thin shoulders and the miles of silence in her world of blame had scarred their marriage, which for a time was an open scab unable to heal. Silence had been her way of stiffening blame toward him. He should have driven Annie home and left the church early that day. He could have held her and never let her go.

One by one, the old mill towns fell away in the distance. A rising mist from the lather of the river disguised them as if they resided in the past, with no future, no glory ahead, only a place in history near the black current of water. He clutched her picture in his shirt pocket beneath his coat, and like a broken reel on an old projector, his mind ticked through all the churches where he'd held it up, breathing life into it, so others could search and pray. Every barn with a cross, every clapboard building with a signpost for Christ, any church that claimed the name of Jesus was a candidate for his cause; the ones who still believed in miracles over nature, miracles over evil, the crazy honest ones who could pull down the heavens in a prayer.

His tires peeled back the snow in the town of Alder Creek. A worn place of stilted homes and cracked foundations. The Christmas lights couldn't hide the sighs of this historic place. Electric snowflakes on light poles blinked at the weary drivers.

Then the town disappeared behind him in a curtain of white. The bold mountain roads waited ahead. Hairpin turns formed from one precipice to another, and the winds tossed cars like matchboxes. He grabbed the steering wheel until the blood drained from his fingers. His eyes blinked hard. He drove through the mountains and bit on his lower lip until blood trickled.

High Falls had a rest area, a cathedral in the mountains where visitors pulled over to view the amazing glacial world—but in the storm there was no view, only a ledge in the wilderness, a dim-lit progression forward where he stopped his car and surveyed his desperate plight. He needed to feel his feet on the ground, gain some composure for the final trek.

He turned off the ignition and listened to the wind howl. Between gusts, he listened to the falling water and imagined that beneath was a place where if his car fell it might hide until spring, he a frozen iceman trapped in a metal coffin. He thought about this as damp perspiration rode up his neck.

Suicide. It dwelled in the recesses of his mind, occasionally emerging to hook him like a claw hammer. His death would look like an accident. Would anyone blame him? Would his wife's depression get any deeper than her present dark cave? Could this be his poetic justice, since it was he who held Annie last before she disappeared around the corner of the church? He wasn't afraid to meet God; he pictured his spirit ascending from the black water, past the white-brushed fir trees and elms. And what should his martyred voice offer God? *I've searched everyplace else, Lord, is she here?*

Climbing from the car, he snagged the tail of his coat on the open door. He unraveled it and swore into the swirling wind, cursing God. He was helpless in this canyon of rocks: a dome of circular wind unable to chart a course. Perilously close to the edge, he thought perhaps he could crawl back into his car and take the ultimate plunge.

Quietly masked, a jeep had intruded his haunt. It spliced through the snow, and lights gathered toward him as his steps faltered in the headache of wind. His thoughts became a poisoned, drunken stupor. What did he see through eyelids frozen, as he squinted, barely seizing shapes with his burning irises? A shadow came toward him and arrested his movements barely soon enough as the steady roar grew ravenous beneath him. As he stumbled and almost fell, he blindly caught with his hands a frozen wooden rail hidden in a layer of snow.

Two
Homeward Grave

When Robert turned from almost falling to his death, he couldn't control the smile that brushed across his face. He was embarrassed to let it escape. But in front of him stood an imperfect Santa with skinny legs and baggy pants, as if a wisp of a man existed inside those clothes. His hat hung limply, slogged in snow, an old man with a true thin white beard. Fortunately, he also possessed a four-wheel-drive jeep.

The frail old Santa approached him with a raspy voice in the wind. "You okay, Mister?"

In that moment, he felt ambushed. He couldn't get comfortable having Santa in on his suicidal thoughts.

He hung on to his black fur hat as he stepped between the old man and the car. "Just been hoping the storm would ease." He spoke the words, a soft white lie, headlong against the howling wind, which felt like an invisible noose.

Santa nodded and tugged hard on his beard, his legs not looking solid, as if he could be lifted away in the storm on the next gust of wind. "Follow me, if ya like?"

"Sure. Why not?"

Robert followed Santa down the winding gorge, his knuckles bleached white around the rib of the wheel, blood drained from his face.

His thick hands wrapped around the steering wheel made him think about how his father would brag about the size of his son's hands; he would blush and hide behind the barn door. But now, more than anything, he wanted to wrap his hands around the throat of the one who took his daughter. He wanted to watch the blood drain from the perpetrator's face, squeeze him like a feverish boil. His mind was no longer on the hearty, firm handshakes of his faithful congregation. His mind was a storm of unruly thoughts.

His father once told him, "You want to know the character of a man, don't study them darn eyes, shake his hand, and get a good look at 'em, that'll tell ya if he's a good man, you betcha."

Squeezing the wheel, Robert saw a ski lift and a Christmas tree farm, a magical, storybook scene, white and crayon-like green. To the right side were the rolling hills near Boonville where he'd grown up. A collapsed red barn taken down by too many rounds of heavy, wet snow sat yards away from a windowless, abandoned house. The place had a gray hickory color to it. "Farmers don't rule this world anymore," he said, talking to himself.

The drifts pounded like drums on his tires, but the clouds scattered, and above him the sun gave rise to hope that the sailing snow would lie down and melt. But a new challenge emerged as he watched the sun gleam off the sparkling green jeep carrying presents to some town, some hospital, some place meant to be. It occurred to him deeply that this man had a mission of his own, a mission for children somewhere. He must take his job seriously to be out here in this mountainous divide. The presents in the jeep's back window gleamed in the sun, setting the ridge of his eyes on fire until his tears attempted to extinguish the burning.

Along the roadside, the evergreen trees of Forestport spiraled above like guardians of a winter kingdom, as if this were a place where mystery unfolded like a winter garden. They were tall, cleanly erected but thickly winged, so that there was an abundant bed of flesh-colored pine needles not buried by the falling snow. The snow itself tripped down like wet frosting on a cake as the sun softened its leavening grip on the prickly branches.

Down this corridor of trees, leading into the final descent, came the bridge. The clouds had broken, scattered from the sun, and Robert saw that the bridge was lime green, phosphorescent. It arched over the swirling Black River, a river that marked the boundary between the loose, rocky mountainous soil and the fertile, sloped farm fields to the east. The snake of a river, black as cobalt, cold as steel, eventually spit its venom into Lake Ontario. One could imagine a day in the ghostly past when the ice-age shelf had retreated, leaving large boulders in pockets of woods, scraped, gouged, and reforming this primitive landscape. Yet the river looked dark and menacing, as if it had a prehistoric hold, as if some scaled reptile thought to be extinct might one day emerge.

Passing over the bridge, the town was marked by a boat shop of ancient wooden masterpieces, carved from the cherry trees of this place with countless coats of lacquer to protect them. The boats were left in the mounds of snow, as if all the years of hand-sweated veneer could not be tarnished.

An old Victorian estate high on a western hill gave the town an anchored character in the winds of change. Its front porch was old-fashioned, accustomed to entertainment in the summer, presently shackled by drifts. Miniature carved edges gave it a regal quality for a clapboard town. This hillside estate included an eleven-room motel, yards off and almost obscured in the background, in hibernation mode until summer when a mighty migration of summer travelers from the big cities like New York would pass through.

Santa barreled through the yellow light. Robert turned toward Dutch Hollow, splitting the road and threading the snow. He flashed his lights to thank him, but the old guy kept his mile-long stare toward the city of Utica and the highway. Santa was on a mission.

The wind eased, giving Robert a chance for a deep, satisfying breath. He pulled a package of Tums from the top of his shirt pocket, but they spilled into his lap. He reached down into his crotch and forked them with his fingers, then chewed them like candy.

From behind the large-pane window in the family room of the old Victorian home, Santa and the pastor had been watched. Skye, the new girl, only ten, had wrapped part of a thick purple curtain around her as she pretended to be a princess, pressing her nose to the cold-fogged window to watch the two drivers tumbling through the intersection. She admired everything about it: the way the tires paddled the snow, the way the snow fell to the sides like white oceanic spray. Most of all she wanted to play in the snow.

She wanted to make a snow angel. She was adopted, from Oklahoma, and the only snow she remembered had quickly melted in a noonday heat. She wished to ask her new mom about her chances for the next day, when she could spread-eagle on her back, innocently winging into the shape of a perfect angel.

Robert Davis saw that the salt had been deposited from trucks, and the steady romp of car traffic had turned the leftover snow into mush. His mind too was a slush pile full of useless leads, beaten down and squashed.

A patch of blue sky formed during his final surge toward home. He passed the Dutch Hollow high school, which looked like a coliseum surrounded by woods. Further down, the red brick of two-story structures marked the center of town. Mimi's Diner was a rectangular building, vanilla white, with an old neon sign, a red coil and a blue coil that spelled "Fish on Friday." The town had passed through the first siege of winter, and Robert felt the clapping of the snow from underneath his car.

Dutch Hollow was a town of bedrooms, a town of community churches, a town not accustomed to strangers.

Life plowed ahead, snow and rain, life and death, the turning of the earth's axis and the leveling of the sun. He wasn't in control of these shortened days, not much more than a robin that builds its nest too low, within arm's length. It could all be swept away, even his job. Life ebbs and flows, and he felt less of himself holding on above the sway.

The last mile took him to the other side of town where his church was perched. He knew he couldn't keep his mind stuck on Annie at age eleven forever. He couldn't hold it all in without bursting, without his cells exploding like fireworks on a cold dry day.

Veteran's Park had a gazebo in its center, and all the community churches including his ribbed around it. Skeleton oak trees, maple too, without a dress for the winter snow, made the place seem void of purpose—as if the churches were empty now. His church, First Presbyterian, had existed on its original slab-and-stone framing since its erection in 1836. It was a place where lonely echoes of his own voice drummed in his ears.

He pretended to hold up his faith in that abandoned well of a sanctuary where the stalwart gathered to be inspired, all forty-five or so congregants, mostly of retirement age, who latched onto each other, starving for immortality. The place had become a nursing ward for the elderly, bundled up to hear Reverend Davis encouraging them to exit into the world and be shredded by the young lions. Be brave, have courage, have faith, none of which this pastor now possessed, and so he felt every Sunday that his message was all phony. God had dealt him a lousy hand, and every week, every sermon was made with a poker face.

The nativity scene was frosted with icicles; Joseph was tilted, almost fallen, and Mary had turned away from Jesus, who himself was almost completely buried in the snow.

A hazed lens in his mind took over the ticks of his memory: his daughter left his control on those steps, then rode her blue bicycle with the face cards pinned to the rims, making the sounds of a twin-engine propeller. He could still see her fading away, noisily turning the corner onto the paved road toward home and disappearing somewhere into an eternal nightmare.

It was only a half-mile, but it could just as easily have been the Bermuda Triangle. Past the graveyard, past the line of trees and the farmer's field to the left, she had disappeared, stolen, green from the vine of life. On his right were a string of sparsely planted houses, country-like and thickly painted. Like his, their lawns slanted uphill and were dotted with oak and white elm. His trek through the winter storm was nearly over, and he could see his house over the ridge, a cold ivory house, where he and his family survived.

He plowed upward into his driveway through fresh snow until his back tires spun to a stop. His entry was silent, stealthy under the radar of his wife. He knew her comfort zone. He imagined her, swallowed in her favorite wicker chair, curled up with crochet needles and yarn. Her face was bleached white from not having been in the sun all year; her hair pulled back, a natural blonde with strands of gray. Mary forced her loss deep inside. She spoke when cornered. The pain only grew when they were forced to confront the subject of Annie together. Their life was a brewing caldron, waiting to spill over until the acidic stew would peel away their flesh.

He turned off the ignition and worked his silence. He spied his son Robbie above in his room. The ten-year-old used his bed for a trampoline. He was growing, edging closer to the age that Annie had been, on his way to manhood. For a moment the pastor and father closed his eyes, and the precious sun warmed his eyelids, small comfort for his daydreams. He imagined, or tried to think of what it was like, where her bike had fallen that hot sunny day, and how it was found in the tall weeds, some of the face cards making those little chirping noises from the wheels spinning in an afternoon breeze. Now here it was next to him, buried in the snow, rusted to the core where he had lain it down after it was delivered without hope from that cursed field.

The snap of the car door made his son look down from his window. It was time for Robert, the father, to put his reverend hat away as he opened the front door with its bell-laden, noisy wreath, creating an air of expectancy. Brushing the snow from his shoulders like thick dandruff, stomping his rubber boots, he bestowed a wealth of stubborn snow on the brown sheet of linoleum. A wooden coatrack conveniently doubled as storage and melting zone for both hat and coat. His nostrils relaxed; he could smell a roast. His eyes blinked and watered in relief.

Little Rob came bounding down the stairs. "Hey, Dad!"

No matter what, he always had a smile for his son. No matter the pain, he could force a smile when he had to.

Mary leaned from the kitchen, a large metal spoon across her chest at a contorted angle. The satisfying smell of a Sunday pot roast drifted over the entry. "Supper's near ready," she said.

He breathed it in.

The dad, the man without a collar or cross, settled in to rub his son's warm and waxen sandy-brown hair. He looked for the soft places—like his son's head or the familiar scents that washed through his nose here—to relieve the tension of this frightful Sunday afternoon.

"Well, little man, get cleaned up for supper."

The phone rang. The family had learned, after all these months, to freeze in place and listen to the answering machine as if it could be news, but not to get too close. Let the machine talk. Let the machine stop time if need be.

But no one could have prepared them for this phone call.

"This is the Davis residence, please leave a message. Your call is important to us." It was Mary's drowning tones on the machine. It used to have

Annie's cheerful voice. They took the tape out and salted it away among her other small possessions, upstairs in a drawer of her room, as if she might want to hear it herself one day when she miraculously walked through the door.

The background noise on the other end of the line sounded like a truck stop, like a pay phone in some transient place. But the voice came on clearly, and remarkably like a librarian, in a low crisp tone. "Ah, if this is the reverend's residence, I…my name is Donna Brushton. I…I have some important information I would like to share with you. If possible, I could come to your office at church and meet with you tomorrow. I don't have a number or anything where you can reach me, but I will look for you. Thanks."

"Crazy!" he blurted out. "I'm supposed to wait for a stranger to show up from the shadows?"

They looked at each other with confusion and surprise, and little Rob shrugged his shoulders. But no one dared stir the cauldron of emotions further, not now, not this time.

Robert knew what he had to do. He had to hide his own rigid reaction when she came around. He had to listen to her world, even if it stepped over his faith. The serious tone was obvious to him on the phone. He suspected she might be a self-professed psychic or medium—more than one had come to him before. This made him uncomfortable, like waiting for someone with magical powers. But then, deep within him, a trembling new excitement for what she might know tugged at his floundering heart.

Three
Snow Castle

Skye, enjoying her first season with snow, kept her nose pressed to the large, framed window of the Taylor house. She enjoyed how the cold conducted through the window and how the air brushed her freckled face. This new world of hers needed to be explored. She hungered to dive into the snow as it glistened like tiny diamonds. Shadows arched over the house, and the sun nestled in the valley west.

She imagined her world a palace, and her new family was a royal dynasty. She had been plucked, rescued from a heroin-laced trailer outside of Oklahoma City, where her mother and father ran tracks up their arms and together contracted AIDS. Her parents did everything together except death. Her mother had screamed from her hospital bed, telling her husband that he had killed her. Her brain was saturated with infection, and she died soon after. Her last words on earth were a chilling cry for her baby.

Her husband, who couldn't be shocked into giving up his own habit, raced across the country using Skye as a pawn to get drugs, preying on church families. When he found a gracious family in the Taylor home, they made him sign her off on a notarized document that she would one day be theirs—never mind the price of his loaded veins. When he died, his own mother worked with the Taylor family to ensure the adoption went forward as hoped.

The fireplace reflected softly in the windowpane as shadows widened over the panoramic setting. A fiery tongue seemed to dance on the oak flooring, and it magnified her imagined stage as she retreated from the window. Even the old Labrador, Abby, ambled into the picture; her thick golden hair glimmering; and suddenly the dog was not so old, but revived.

Skye spied her new mother down the hall in the kitchen, carrying on multiple duties. Jane, once a high school gymnast, had nearly qualified for the Olympics as a teen, but now she kept most of her flexibility by restoring the large old house, minding the motel, and caring for the new baby. Drew sat firmly in his high chair, beating his plastic tray with wooden spoons meant to keep him occupied. He had not yet found a smooth rhythm.

Skye strolled down the hall, feeling the polished wood on the balls of her stocking feet. Her thin pink gown reflected in the hardwood, which now looked to her as a sea of glass. With the dancing of the fireplace, there were waves at her feet. She steadily moved toward the kitchen, helped along by the reflective wave of the floor.

Jane moved her limbs delicately, nothing unused, from the curl of her bare toes angling open the hood of the oven to the amazing twists and contortions performed to put away dishes. This was her world, and she could make it dance or sing.

"Mom," Skye persisted over the slap of dishes and Drew's constant drumming. "Mom!"

Jane twirled around and landed into Skye.

"Skye! I didn't hear you, girl." Jane bent over and clutched Skye's shoulders to steady herself. Her mousy-brown hair brushed the girl's face. "Careful, honey, I'm in a hurry to get dinner ready for Joe. He's working those long hours at the wire plant."

"Can I healp?" Skye asked with a southern twang.

"Okay, pass me the clean dishes from the other side of the sink."

"Mom." Skye loved how it sounded, how it fell off her lips as a universal word that could stop the rotation of the earth. Finally, it stopped Jane's whirlwind of motion.

"What, Skye?"

"Can I make a snow angeal?"

"Tomorrow is a school day."

"How 'bout if there's no school ?"

"I guess. Better wrap yourself up like a mummy."

A wide smile streaked across Skye's face.

"First things first. We'll see if school closes."

"For real?" Skye squealed, dancing on the toes of her feet and clasping her hands together.

An hour later, Joe Taylor came home and headed in sidelong through the door, brushing off the snow. A shivering, thin man, he lived with a worried line across his brow.

They ate dinner and then snuggled together on the couch in front of the television and fireplace. The snow outside had eased Joe's weary look, piling on a sense of insulation and separation from the everyday world. He stretched on the couch into a deep sigh. His eyes grew heavy until he broke into a slight snore.

That evening Skye ambled up the stairs, and faithful Abby wagged her tail and followed in pursuit. The stairs were narrow, with only a subfloor, and each step sounded like the twisting of branches in the wind. Warm air gushed into the attic bedroom.

Skye shook the covers and rolled into bed. She found a satisfied peace beneath her patchwork quilt. Sleepy-eyed, she managed to mumble a prayer, asking God to spare the stars their work and let more clouds roll in. Her eyelids grew heavy until they closed like thick velvet curtains.

Suddenly, waves of light raced into her window, which overlooked the motel rooms. Abby lifted her head anxiously and then cowered down between her front paws. The dog's cold nose brushed Skye's loose fingers. She jerked her hand and rolled over.

That night, she dreamed of her mother. Her mom had a zipper for a mouth and couldn't open it. Her eyes were black, matching the mascara that ran down her bone-thin face. She looked like a scarecrow. She called for her daughter to follow her as she drifted past the frosted pines in the dark of night. But Skye sank into the snow up to her thighs. She wanted to keep stride, but her feet were heavy mallets. Eventually she lost sight of her mother's sunken, ghostly face, a face that held an unspoken warning.

Four

Snow Cave

The Davis house was a fortress from the storm as evening fell. A firmament of clear, pointed stars spread light over the imperial white landscape. Their house, too, guarded by tall oak trees and blanketed by snow, brought them a sense of insulation—a buffer in the evening from the world.

Robert and Mary kept to their evening rituals. She sat erect in front of the mirrored dresser, combing down unruly strands of gray. He was reading a book by C.S. Lewis—*Pilgrim's Regress,* the story of a boy in search of an illusive island that holds the key to the universe.

During preparation for bed in the upstairs master bedroom, they hardly spoke or made eye contact. Mary continued to work the strands of her hair, as if pain was important to her and would make her strong. Fried gray at the edges, she leaned into her mirror from the vanity now and then, revealing a look at her husband propped stiffly in their king bed, reading. He sensed her eyes watching him from the mirror. "So what do you suppose this woman will tell you?" she said.

Robert felt the whip of her deliberate words and reached for something to say, stumbling on thin air, waiting for his voice to work with his lips. "I suppose it's nothing. If it was I would have heard it from the sheriff." He went back to reading, walking on a journey with a boy named John, seeking the island that eluded him.

"Shouldn't I be there?" she asked.

He pulled down his reading glasses, a deep furrow in his brow. "And listen to some crackpot?"

"But you will," she declared.

"Well, I can't bar the door of the church."

If her defensive walls were in the home, his were in his church; it was his way to barricade himself from the everyday world, hiding like a self-righteous monk, daring anyone to find him.

He saw no words of encouragement forming in her mouth. She rose from her chair biting her thin lips, shuffling toward the bed. Her white gown was yellowed where it scratched the floor like old parchment.

She turned her lamp off and joined him from the other side, allowing a sliver of cold to form between them in bed. He glanced back to her. She stared toward the mirror as if she longed to disappear inside of it. Perhaps she wanted a nonrefundable *Alice in Wonderland* trip. Her catatonic shuffling through the house, her deliberate distance in bed—she clearly did not want to be here.

Robert felt the snowplow shake the foundation of the house. Pulsating lights found their way across their darkened room. They lay tucked in bed, tilted in opposite directions. He, tied only by the covers, hung on the edges of loneliness and guilt. The sounds of the snowplow engine and heavy metal scraping an icy road entered the room. The steel-bladed monster consumed what it could not repel.

Robert's eyes grew heavy, and he slipped into the underworld, the one between what is real and imagined, a place where his little girl was hiding. In his fractured mind, she held her favorite Cabbage Patch doll at the doorway, a lighted silhouette from the hall. He couldn't trace a smile on her face, only a distant impression, like a shadow of something once vibrant, moving, alive, but now ghostly, surreal.

He unfurled the covers tightly bound over his feet so his mind would not think he was fitted for a coffin, and he released himself to sleep, his mind tumbling into the void of a welcomed, dreamless state.

Five
Cold Fever

I t was before dawn's first light. Robert made sure not to disturb his wife's sleep. He listened for her heavy breathing, the kind that whistled and built with momentum as air exhaled from the back of her throat and through her nose. He knew sleep had taken her deep into the riptide of her own perilous dreams.

He shifted toward the cold, dank floor.

The roar of the furnace came through the floor vents, injecting his nostrils with oily fumes. He staggered from his stupor in long johns that rode up his knees and stabbed in the darkness for the bathroom light until its yellow flickering beam radiated over him.

There was a ringing in his ears and grit in his red, swollen eyes. He dug into them until he could see his face in the mirror. He felt a dull pain to the side of his head, and the ringing in his ears made him search for his marching legs. As he wrestled to strip off his skivvies, he was helpless as a fragile animal in a crate until he found deliverance in the shower where hot beads of water pounded his feeble flesh. He felt blood like hot metal clearing his mind and awakening his limbs.

After dressing in black, he crept past his wife's body without offering a kiss or a prayer. The house was doused in the slim film of darkness. He managed to find his boots, coat, and hat, then angled his way out the snow-bound door into the cold and silver-gray horizon. A slap of air stiffened his nostrils and widened his eyes. Bundled in his coat and firmly in his car, he turned the key and revved the engine to find momentum against the parked plateau of his driveway, then skirted down toward the pale street lamps in town, toward his church on the edge of town.

He punished the snow with his wheels near the steps of the church and quickly darted from his car, creating cookie-cutter impressions in the white crust. The church's red door with its hanging Christmas wreath was an easy target in a landscape that had shifted from blowing snow in the night. He turned the key until the door reluctantly opened.

It was good to be inside his domain, and he felt a satisfied self-pity at being alone. It was here that he could scoff at the world from his perch deep inside. Since Annie had disappeared, his purpose in the church was not to build a bridge to suffering souls, but a sanctuary. A selfish wall of privacy, a solitary grief—a hiding place.

He pushed against the door to close it. A wedge of snow caught the threshold, and the bells on the wreath shook. He leaned against it with an unforgiving grunt until it finally closed.

Darkness etched the sanctuary and the hard-backed pews. As he walked the side aisle, only a faint light appeared through the stained-glass windows, enough to enable him to walk half-blind toward his office. The air thickened with the absence of life. It felt more like a museum than a church, a place of artifacts and historical markers. How could anyone serve in a parish like this? *My chamber of grief,* he mused.

He found the switch on his wall. Low-hanging fluorescent lights buzzed, then winked in brightness. Placing his hat and coat on the rack in the corner, he turned to face his desk, empty of true work but piled with books, stacked and leaning. His agenda was a resignation letter, one he had attempted to complete for days. A chicken-wire basket overflowed with scrunched papers.

He sat in his cold leather chair, which had wheels with a bad sense of direction. He bent and struggled to pull the chair forward until at last he was comfortably alone on his clerical throne.

Beams of light cascaded through curtainless windows. The sun reigned supreme. But it only made him feel exposed, targeted by an unseen world. The false light above was no match for the rising angle of the sun, and it seemed only to magnify the depth of cold.

Ancient floor pipes rattled out heat, but his body shook, chilled. The old office absorbed the warmth before his flesh could.

He pulled the Tums from his shirt pocket, and a few rolled out along his desk like loose change. He attempted to catch them on the old oak desk-top; some landed close to his daughter's carved initials before he snatched them up. It had been a place where Annie and her younger brother played, spinning on his chair until dizzy, filling up the archaic office with a depth of innocence, a robust sphere of unchained love. He sighed for what once was.

His office was a history of paintings and photographs from different generations. The church had several black-and-white photos of pastors who had served there, dating back to when Abraham Lincoln was president. All were lined along a ribbed parchment- colored wall, and no matter which way he turned, they kept their eyes toward him, and he was a part of them.

The town itself was founded shortly after the American Revolution when the Protestant churches each built their own places of worship. Before that time, the grange hall served a community of farmers for all social events, including church services. But that was when family farms dominated the landscape.

Churches soon sprang up, lining up beside each other, a testament to distinction and diversity while maintaining a spirit of cooperation.

The Presbyterian church had not lost its Calvinist leanings, and his wall of the faithful eyed him carefully as he progressed through his pain and sought the miracle of deliverance for Annie. He wasn't so sure his stern-looking brothers on the wall would like his next visitor. The grace of God kept his congregation pure, but this one visitor could shake its foundation.

The pastor did his best to imagine the proper professional pose to take with his mysterious guest. But no matter what he did, from the height of the vaulted ceiling in his office to the frame of his large oak desk, the room and all of its trappings made him feel less than his modest five feet, ten inches.

As the sun took hold of a snow-encrusted landscape, steady drips of ice melted from the gutter. Gleaming ice mounds formed where the water slipped down. The rhythm of those droplets drummed in his brain. He ran his fingers through his thick black hair until his hands cupped the cavity of his ears.

Suddenly, she was outside his office. He shifted back in his chair and felt a current of nervous anticipation dampen his face. This short brick of a woman filled his doorway. His heart shuddered. Donna Brushton had somehow managed to walk stealthily from the entry door to Robert's office, even along the hard-back pews in the sanctuary.

As she breached the door to his office under the bold lights, it seemed as if dust particles were alive in the darkness behind her. When she spoke, her flushed red lips hardly moved in the confines of a small, tight mouth. Her face was porcelain white and her skin tight as if melted or molded to her round face. "Reverend," she said, letting her tongue cleave to the "d" sound.

She waited as if on stage, a curtain call for her captive audience. Her voice was calculated, measured for just the correct effect in his moment of quiet anticipation.

He cranked back from his chair and used his elbows in a valiant attempt to be seen and heard above the leaning tower of his books. "So, you're Donna, the one who called last night?"

"Yes, I'm Donna. Um…Donna Brushton." She moved forward, revealing her gray wool jacket. Stepping pigeon-toed and close between the walls of books, her eyes came into focus with his. They were the color of dark chocolate.

"You're a smart man, Reverend. You surround yourself with books."

"Paper education is not all it's cracked up to be." He gathered his wits. "Would you like fresh coffee? Sometimes it makes me a better listener, besides chasing away the chill."

She kept her eyes pressed to him, but he looked away to the wall of his predecessors.

"You believe in gifts, don't you, sir?"

He fidgeted in his chair. "Well, we might agree that we are all endowed with certain gifts," he said with a forced smile.

"Sir, coffee does sound like the perfect thing to chase away the chill."

"Make yourself as comfortable as possible in one of my old chairs. I think they came with the founders. I'll be back when you can hear the coffee sing."

He stood up beside her and offered to take her coat, but she shook off his gesture. He stepped around her and with another forced smile said, "Call me pastor. Reverend is for weddings and funerals."

And for a moment, he felt his wit had caught her by surprise, as if he had not lost the ability to turn a conversation in his favor. He was more than a man of cloth, a man of clever words.

But it was the father in him crying from inside, not the reverend, who sought to make her feel just comfortable enough, perhaps special enough to say something, anything that might bring him closer to finding Annie.

This visit, her unusual gift, was a bruise to his faith. *Why not just ask the devil where she is?* He needed to leave and fix the coffee, to gather strength and pray like a man in hell who needs ice.

This meant a retreat to the stale old kitchen, which hadn't seen a makeover in nearly thirty years. The ancient linoleum floor was yellowing, curled, and soiled along the edges.

He was prepared to ask her why. Why, if she had information, hadn't she contacted Sheriff Brower? He struck a match along the ridge of the stove and watched as a blue flame circled to life. He poured water into the metal coffeepot, meditating, praying weakly, thinking about Annie as he stared through the kitchen window. His mind wandered, lost somewhere beyond the ice-layered creek. Finally, the coffee whistled, simmered, and slipped along the silvery sides of the pot.

He hid the hammering in his heart, his chest burning as if acid had dripped from every word that hung from the corner of her tight mouth. And she hadn't yet told him anything. He didn't want her to know it; he didn't want her to feel his anxiety; not if she just wanted some attention. He wouldn't let her put one knowing finger on his bleeding heart.

Donna stood in the office, running her fingers over the old Haitian cotton chairs with high, uncomfortable-looking backs and flowers that looked like faded watermelons.

She shuffled her fat white legs around his desk, drawn to the hen scratches from his children on the old desk where their initials were carved. She traced their names with the tip of her trembling index finger. She ran her fingers over the *A,* over the *n,* and over the next *n,* as if they were Braille. She was reading with her mind, closing her eyes, her eyelids fluttering as if butterflies were relaying coded information into her brain.

Her finger trembled in the air. Her body seemed to be suspended by invisible stage wires, and her eyes suddenly sprang open, caught on an invisible hook.

When he returned, it was his turn to stand in the doorway of his office. She had walked toward the bright light of the window. It occurred to her that this was his private chamber—he did not ordinarily leave even the patrons of his church there alone. "Reverend, sir, I'm afraid your daughter is near dark waters. She's alone. She's very alone."

"But alive?" He stood with coffee cups shaking in each hand.

She said nothing, and a heavy silence fell.

"But she's alive. Right?"

"Sorry. No. I…I can't say. I…I can't say for now." She turned to him, this time with an unsteady approach and an ashen face. She awkwardly maneuvered past him.

"You can't just do this. You can't just walk in here and spew a few words from your mouth, then leave." He watched her walk down the aisle to the door, her dark boots shimmering in deliberate strides. He set the cups on the edge of his desk and shouted into the deep sanctuary, "So this is how you help someone?"

She creaked open the front door. The light blinked back.

"Where can I find you? Where can the authorities find you?" But his words weighed heavy and fell in the gray void. The door closed behind her and the light was gone.

He walked past the empty pews and down the hall as if it were his gangplank. He opened the door, letting the cold air rake his nostrils. The sun boiled his eyes. Her black ankle boots had left tracks leading to Mimi's Diner on the corner. And he knew then that she was staying in one of the apartments above the hometown restaurant.

"So she likes to play god, does she?" His chest rattled as he coughed up phlegm.

Six

Snow Angel

Midmorning sun prevailed against high, thin clouds, finding Skye Taylor's attic window. Her eyelids shuddered open, and she remembered, deep in the haze of her mind, that school might just be closed.

She stumbled down the stairs, with Abby close on her heels, wagging her tail. Buckles from her pink snowsuit slapped the almond stairs like the crack of a whip.

Joe Taylor had left early for work, about sunrise, glad to have his four-wheel-drive pickup truck. He had squared the car in his own tracks last night, and today he easily knifed down the sloping hill. Before he left, he noticed what appeared to be an abandoned car but didn't think much more of it. The icy road conditions would already make him late for work. It was an old, powder-blue seventies car, a Ford, he thought, and it seemed matchbook-sized compared to the high plowed banks. No one appeared to be inside, and he hadn't time to play scout.

Skye spotted Jane on the couch with baby Drew. As she approached, the baby was riding on a hypnotic wave of Jane's labored breathing. Skye announced her entry with loose, clanging buckles. The fireplace flickered with embers and ashes, and the hardwood floor kept a cool waxen glow as the sun lighted through the window and absorbed the darkness of the room. She stood in front of Jane and tugged on her shoulder.

Jane, hung over from a lack of sleep, mumbled the words that Skye hoped to hear. "No school today, hon." She adjusted herself more securely on the couch with the baby.

Skye walked over and peered through the frosted picture window where she had pressed her nose the night before. Uninvited snow drifted onto the front porch, covering the legs of wicker chairs like arctic dunes.

She stumbled down the hall to the breezeway for her other garments: a white hat with a red hanging ball, red mittens, and her ocean-blue coat. Abby excitedly followed her every step, sniffing the cool air that filtered through the cracks of the door.

The freckles on Skye's face nearly vanished in her smile while she found her boots littered among the others. She fell backward into the corner as she pulled each boot on with a grunt. Abby licked her face.

The breezeway faced the hibernating motel. Abby scratched on the inside door, and Skye opened it. After that, the screen moved with a nudge from the dog's nose. Abby took off, plowing through the snow, creating a rabbit trail. When she returned, she was dusted from snout to tail.

Skye wanted to play with Abby, but that was secondary to making the perfect snow angel, something she had wanted to do her whole life. She thought for a moment as she pulled her knit cap down over her ears. "Abby, I'll come getcha later, girl. Gotta make me an angeal first."

Abby turned a snow-cone nose toward the motel. She barked as if she could sniff a mouse in hiding.

"Don't you worry, girl, you'll get your turn." Skye allowed Abby the freedom to explore her father's fresh tire tracks in the driveway. For a moment Abby hesitated, perched in the snow, and then she pounced, digging into it until her nose was all white. Then she seemed startled and looked toward the motel rooms on the horizon, as if something was out there. She retreated and ran back to Skye in the breezeway, attempting to lick her face, but this time Skye was ready. "Okay, Abby! Okay, enough!"

Skye shooed the dog inside and imagined the drumroll of a magical moment. She hooked the breezeway door tight so that Abby was unable to push it open. After all, she didn't want the dancing excitement of her dog to ruin an angel creation.

The virgin snow was beautiful, and some trickled down her sleeve, burning her exposed wrist. Skye tasted it; it melted on her tongue. She fell into it. She rolled in it.

Seeking the perfect place to make a snow angel, she sliced between the house and the motel. The stretch was inviting and desolate.

She didn't know that a stranger watched her—she an unexpected gift to be seized in the moment, a fallen green apple to be taken and ripened in his own lair.

As she lay down spread-eagled, arms and legs scissoring back and forth, a strange shadow grew over her. It was not a cloud, but a man, with bent yellow teeth, glasses taped at the bridge, and a fearsome smile.

Abby barked in the breezeway, and it woke Jane up. She tumbled from the edge of the couch. She secured the baby, pressing pillows along the edge. Abby didn't stop barking—and she only yelped when she had good reason.

Jane checked the clock over the mantel; it was nearly nine-thirty. She walked down the hall and into the breezeway.

"Whatsa matter, Abby girl?" she said. "Need to go out?"

Abby raced out, dipped her nose in the snow, and pouted.

Jane folded her arms and stood on the balls of her stocking feet, shaking from the cold. "Skye! You out there?"

Nothing.

Abby dashed over to the side of the house where the snow angel marked the white ground, but she ran back to Jane alone, covered in snow.

Jane opened the screen and craned her neck. She saw footprints toward the drive and toward the left too, toward the side of the house, and even up by the motel.

"Skye!" She cupped her hands. A hawk circled above, flying solo, creating *caw* sounds between her shrills.

Jane went inside and up the stairs through the house, then down to the basement. With each step into another lifeless room, her pace quickened. Her stomach felt emptied as if in the downward spiral of a coaster ride.

She stepped into her boots, tossed on her coat, and went straight outside, turning toward the motel and cupping her hands to her mouth. "Skye! Skye!" Bitter cold dried her throat until it felt like some small animal clawing her from the inside every time she called her daughter's name. "Skye!"

Panic closed on Jane's face and became a mask of horror. Her raspy voice reverberated down the drive through the woods, along a deserted road in front of her. Thoughts of Annie Davis and her disappearance snipped at her mind, following her with every anxious step.

She turned from the drive up the hill and saw Abby between the house and the motel. "Where is she, Abby?" She cut through thigh-deep snow, angling for the dog, who turned in small circles. Her hands were numb, her vocal cords scratched. She spoke to Abby with a charred voice. "Where is she, girl?"

Jane looked down on the snow angel, pristine, as if someone or something had lifted Skye from a near-perfect indention. The snow next to it was ruffled and marred where Skye had played, no tracks standing out. An avalanche of emotions tumbled down from her mind to her heart. She turned toward the motel and could see large booted footprints leading to a room. Gaping prints led down the hill and to the road, but she wanted to believe that Skye was hiding in the room. She desperately clung to the hope that Skye was in there.

Number six wasn't locked, but slightly ajar. As Jane approached the storm door, her nose stiffened at the smell of stale cigarettes.

She meekly called out her name. "Skye?"

Walking inside, she scanned the room. It was obvious that someone had spent the night. The bedspread was ruffled. The picture on the wall hung unevenly. When Jane opened the closet, the air shot forward damp and heavy. Only darkness appeared. She pulled back the bathroom door. Her eyes widened over an uplifted toilet full of cigarette butts sloshed in urine. It made her nostrils flare and her head spin. She stood shivering in a cold, disheveled room.

She stooped to vomit, but nothing came up.

She raced outside, going from door to door at the motel, shouting Skye's name until her throat burned. At every door, she stumbled through the snow, exhausted, listening, but she only heard a high-arching hawk in a steel-blue sky.

Abby followed Jane into a few of the rooms but then darted into the snow, creating large circles and sometimes getting buried out of sight. This caused Jane to focus, pause, and look down at the tracks that seemed to fall off the edge of the world. Deep in her bruised and beaten heart, she knew that Skye, her little princess, was gone. She couldn't protect her, and the snow wasn't a barrier to evil.

She trudged through the snow far enough to see the reality of her nightmare. No car, but fresh tire tracks. Wet sniffles dribbled down her reddened nose. Sore tears streaked from her eyes.

Racing uphill through the snow, with every ounce of her being she pulled the storm door so hard in the breezeway that it bent off the hinges and slapped back, warped for good. She reached for the phone in the kitchen, leaking snow everywhere, and as she dialed, she could hear the baby crying with hearty lungs.

The call: 911. "What's your emergency?"

"I think my daughter's been kidnapped!"

"Your daughter's been taken, ma'am?" A surreally calm voice crackled on the line.

"Please! Please! I live at 102 Route 28 in Forestport!"

"We're alerting the nearest car to your location. Please tell me what happened. Why are you sure?"

Drew was crying hysterically, and Jane heard the sound of his body tumbling to the floor from the couch.

"Is that the missing child crying?"

"No! No! It's my baby, I have to get him." Tears sprang from Jane's face, and she attempted to wipe them on her jacket. She dropped the phone and rushed to Drew, settling him on her shoulder. The receiver twirled on the floor from a long cord in the kitchen.

"An officer is on the way, ma'am. Can you hear me?"

The state police officer had been checking out an abandoned car only a few miles away when he answered the call.

Abby barked at the police car approaching up the drive. The officer's broad hat emerged from the car door while the red lights silently flashed. Wrapped in his parka, he quickly shuffled through the snow to the main door of the parlor. Jane saw him and let the receiver go again. "It's my daughter, she's gone, she's gone!"

"Okay, tell me why you're sure and where you think she might be." The trooper watched Jane pacing back and forth.

"She…she was outside. There were tracks. And…and I found out someone broke into one of our motel rooms."

Concern raked his face, and he called in for help. "See any cars, descriptions?"

"She was outside just for a minute, and next thing I know, she's…she's gone! And…and all these tracks down to the road? She's gone! She's gone!" Jane stopped and looked straight at him without blinking. "I think I'm gonna throw up." But once again, nothing came out as she dipped forward with the baby against her side.

"Can we put the baby in his playpen and go outside for a minute?"

Jane's hands trembled as she released the baby, but he had stopped crying.

"Who else lives here? Where is your husband?"

"He's at work."

"Could he have taken…"

"No! No! He left early, and she was with me."

She went outside and showed him the tracks. Another police car pulled up. The officers talked. One left down the road, attempting to follow the fresh tire tracks. The other police officer headed north on Route 28.

Joe heard the intercom tell him to report to the office. The boss had a bag phone, the best portable for service where cell towers were few. He yelled at Joe when he heard the news. "Here!" He threw the bulky phone at him. "Call me on it when you find her."

Jane led the original officer to the motel room, number six. She paced in front of him while he got back on his talkie and asked for someone in forensics to come out. But it would be a good hour; the nearest lab was in Utica near the thruway. Meanwhile, he reassured Jane that he'd find Skye—but she knew that was a promise only God could make. Together they unlocked all the rooms and did an entire sweep of the area until more police cars arrived.

As Joe Taylor drove from the wire factory in Camden with the bag phone in the passenger seat of his truck, he remembered the car: a light-blue one, seventies, rusted, maybe a Ford Fairmont. It had seemed to be abandoned, and the reality slammed his mind—it would be easy for someone to split a lock on one of the motel rooms and spend the night in seclusion, waiting for the storm to pass. The thought of what he had earlier dismissed on his way to work, and the grave possibility that a stranger might have his daughter, made the hair on his neck rise. He punished himself with one particular thought. *Why didn't I just write down the license plate?*

An empty blue sky in front of him and the sun reflecting from the snowbanks made driving more difficult. Joe grabbed for the phone, not used to calling from a vehicle, and attempted to get the house phone so he could give the police his information. The reception crackled.

Jane grabbed the receiver on the first ring. What Joe knew was relayed to an officer with a pad and pencil, who talked down to his shoulder where the radio was pinned to his vest. The wheels of every available uniformed agency came to life as the officer passed information through invisible currents.

Jane's world clung to those electronic signals.

Electrical wire kept the trunk tied down where the keyhole should've been. Rust had eaten this car until the lock was decayed and useless. Skye had been knocked out with the force of a steel jack, but he duct-taped her, hog-style, for good measure. Tape stretched across her mouth, just in case she woke up before he brought her to her new home in the woods.

The bruise on her forehead turned shades of purple and green. Her dirty blonde hair twisted and snarled with tire chains and rotten pieces of fender. A warm pool of blood settled between her sticky head and a tire iron, which had been used to prod her body in case she was faking being knocked out.

When the abductor climbed a steep grade, blue smoke funneled from the carburetor, drifting under the car until it surfaced behind them as a cancerous cloud over Route 28.

Her coat was shredded, boots dangling from her feet.

Skye breathed through her wet nostrils, and the stiffness of cold sifted through her mind, so cold it burned the memory of where she'd been sealed shut. Her eyelids danced, her mind wanting to lift and survey her world. When her eyes lightened and her eyelids sprang up, she gave a faint muffled cough through the duct tape, and the horror of where she'd been placed flashed through her mind. Suddenly her stomach felt as if she was being carved from the inside.

Although Skye's head pounded in pain, she peeked through the open keyhole and could see a car behind them, a sliver of hope to hold in her tortured mind, until it drew so close she was lost in darkness again.

Seven
Snow Bound

The abductor, wearing a crooked smile and uneven glasses, scanned a remote parking space at the Grab Bag Mini-Mart. He was at a fork in the road beneath the mountains.

Before heading inside, he checked on his living merchandise in the trunk.

Skye spied through the broken keyhole, which formed her only hope of resurrection. Her body was wound tight. Her mouth taped, hands and feet pig-tied, she couldn't do much but squirm in cold fear in the rusted trunk.

Suddenly an eye closed over her only light of hope. "Hi, darling. Don't move or try anything, or I might have to tie you up in the cold snow and let the wolves come have a lick. Deal?"

She played dead as her heart slid into her throat. She peeked below her eyelids, and the light was back. He was gone.

She closed her eyes and swallowed a waxen ball of fear. She wanted to kick the trunk open but couldn't. Twisting and turning her wrist, she felt some slack. Her head throbbed; her stomach soured.

Why me? she thought. *I've been a good girl. Why, God? Why?* She knew her adopted family loved her, and people must be searching for her. Couldn't anybody see her, when she could see people in the distance walking? Through tear-stained eyes, she saw the legs of people walking across the packed snow of the parking lot.

The cold shakes started. Tremors rose from the core of her body.

The abductor stumbled through the door, and a bell clanged from the top. He smelled like mildew and pee, and whenever he bent over or brushed up alongside people in the convenience store, their nostrils perked and he drew sidelong stares.

He found cupcakes in a package and an assortment of sugar products, and his favorite, pepperoni beef sticks. At the cash register, his bills tripped from his pocket to the floor. As he stooped to retrieve them, he gave the blonde girl at the register a hungry grin.

She avoided eye contact and kept her head down as he turned to leave with a full bag of snacks. He stomped toward the door with his long black boots.

In Skye's few moments of hope, her eyes darted for something that could make her free. Her darkness was too close. She managed to feel the rough edges of the jack like a dull knife, and she worked the back of her body against it until the duct tape started shredding from her wrist, strand by strand.

His eye covered the hole again. She closed her eyes, feeling as if she'd been stabbed in the heart. She pretended to be dead but felt that her warm breath could be seen.

Back at the register, the blonde looked through the mini-mart's window and watched the man's strange behavior. He seemed to be talking into his trunk. Her mind wavered, and she wanted to make a mental note, maybe jot down the license plate, but it was covered in hardened snow, and she could hardly make out a number or a letter. People were lined up in front of her, and she left it alone.

The Ford chugged north on the next incline. The abductor watched through his rearview mirror as a pillar of blue smoke formed behind his car. He smacked his legs together while driving as he chewed down one of his beef sticks. Excitement and intensity grew within him; this was the ultimate thrill ride.

Skye sniffed the fumes, fearing she might pass out. But every time she nodded off, the uneven snow-packed road would keep her alert. She'd been through many knocks in her past life, but nothing like this. She was once left abandoned for days in a closed warehouse in Oklahoma, waiting for her father to return with enough money to fix the car and hit the road. Her father's crackhead friends had taken turns molesting and abusing her on the pretense of checking in on her welfare. Things had turned around, and now she had a family, a real family that made her feel special and protected. She blamed herself for the man taking her. She wiped her runny nose into her cold jacket, and salted tears dried on her face. She'd never been this cold, and she couldn't stop shaking.

Her mind raced and whirred through scenarios—how she could get loose, and when he opened the trunk, run for it. She had learned early in life how to run and how to hide.

He knew where he was going, but getting deep enough in the woods and down the old logging road wouldn't be easy. He'd taken advantage of the motel and hadn't intended to bring company with him. She was a temptation he couldn't resist, a piece of candy within his reach. The snowstorm had blocked his way on the roads the night before, making it an impossible feat to get to his hiding place in the woods. With mounds of snow crowned by the sun, it looked deceptively easy to make it today—nature was shining on his adventure.

In his review mirror, he could see roadblocks forming at the intersection he had just passed. Pulsating lights of police cruisers splashed over the frozen white landscape toward the store.

As he drove past unsuspecting cars, he felt the adrenaline rushing through his veins. He was proud of himself that he could walk in and buy groceries with a live girl in his trunk. He nearly peed himself in the exciting flood of thoughts. He was only minutes from his private chamber in the snow.

He turned on Hanson Road about twenty miles north of Forestport, a winding corridor with tall pine trees flanking him on either side, until the road dipped down a ridge with a bridge over a small creek. He wound his way, sometimes spinning tires, until the road flattened back out near railroad tracks and Hanson's Rock Quarry. After passing the railroad tracks, he drove through the forest that grew taller on both sides. Majestic pines created deepening shadows over the white road. When he came to the dead-end turn of an unnamed logging road, where the snowplow had circled earlier, it became clear that the logging road would be a hard charge forward.

A few well-placed cabins dotted the road, and their A-frames revealed ready avalanches of fresh snow about to crash to the forest floor. At times, a scant view through skeleton hardwood trees showed the slice of an outline of Snowbird Lake.

Skye felt the car slow—she nearly had the last piece of tape free from her hands. Her lungs felt heavy. Finally, she loosed her hands and unraveled the tape from her legs. The car jolted her. Her head banged against metal. The car spun, and she could hear its belly scrape the snow. She heard the tires spin, then whine in the cold air.

The kidnapper mulled over an abandoned trailer with shotgun holes sparkling in the sun. A blue tarp hung over a sagging roof. It was a place where he could enjoy her flesh. No one should be within miles. No one would hear her bleating cries. But he wanted to try to get the car where he could use it later. He didn't want to chance leaving it stuck. It would be hidden enough for now. He approached the trunk with a confident stride in the dead of winter.

He untied the wiring, blew on his hands, and opened the trunk. She looked unconscious, and he hoped she wasn't dead—that would spoil everything. But the tremors started and gave her away. She wasn't dead yet. "Peek-a-boo! Stay where you are!" He poked her with his index finger as if he was checking the texture of a raw steak.

She stayed in a fetal position. He smirked at her useless attempt to play dead.

He scratched the stubble of his face and then grabbed the chains from under her body. He closed the hood, but it sprang back slightly.

Skye blinked her eyes open and saw a slice of horizon, fallen trees in the snow, large swaths of pine trees, and a sliver of blue sky.

She heard the chains fall to the ground. Her heart skipped.

When the engine started, she pulled the duct tape from her mouth, swallowed the fumes, and coughed hard. But she knew this was her chance. She kicked open the trunk so hard and fast that it bounced back, ripping off her coat as she tumbled into the snow. She sprang forward, stumbling on dead trees, eyes darting in fear for a way of escape.

Unexpectedly, he stood in the clear path of the road behind them, legs spread, twirling his chains, blocking her easy way out. She had nowhere else to run but down a deer path. As she turned, her wet burning eyes saw what looked like a clearing. *Find the opening and shout!* It seemed too good to be true—a place to run and scream.

Then she heard his foul mouth, chuckling, as he said it. "Hey, doll, don't go down there. That there is Snowbird Lake." He was taunting her. But she didn't dare look back. She just ran toward the opening.

Eight
Thin Ice

S kye tripped face-first in the snow, losing her last boot under a log. Her feet soaking wet and her heart pounding in her chest, she ran the twisted deer path to the clearing. And then she knew—a thin, frozen lake was her only way out of hell.

The child thief knew her fleeting freedom would soon end. A roller coaster of thrills thundered in his veins. He knew the lake, barely frozen, couldn't hold a rabbit. He savored the moment, letting her have a head start. Then, charging like a wolf after his prey, he sliced through the snow.

Branches broke behind her. She turned with holy terror etched into her face as he leaned against a tree and smiled with hungry eyes.

"You won't make it."

He called out, coaxing his wounded animal back to the trap. "Be a good girl, come back. I promise not to hurt ya. I just want to play."

Smoke clouds leaped into the sky from a single cabin across the lake. Her heart sang with hope. *Someone is out here. Someone can hear me cry!*

She looked down at the veil of snow covering the deceptive ice.

"You'll be sorry, doll." She heard his labored breath.

No time. It's run or die.

She slid down the bank; snow filled the back of her shirt and ran up her pant legs. "Help!"

An empty echo raced across the white-scarred lake.

Her feet touched the edge, thin like glass, brushed by snow. Her knees slammed the ice and she heard a *crack.*

"See, I told you!"

Mad with fear, Skye stood up. The ice didn't break. She glared back.

He dove over the bank to get her. His legs punctured the edge and ice water engulfed him to his knees, drenching his boots.

Paddling the snow with her stocking feet, burning cold, her legs drove her forward, ignited by fear. An icy grave lurked below. A cold dark swell of current swept through this belly of water.

Snowbird Lake, made from a dam, had long since flooded an ancient part of this swamp forest. A mangled history of deciduous waste was buried in black water that rose on the heels of a creek with a current that kept ice from growing strong.

Skye kept running; her legs pulsed with adrenaline until she could smell the wood smoke from the A-frame cabin.

In the middle of the lake, the old trunk of a dead tree stuck through the ice. She grabbed it and looked back, watching him crouch, shifting his weight. Twenty yards away, he hesitated.

She caught her breath. Her lungs burned, and the cold air stabbed her ribcage.

Hunched over where the wind swept the ice, she caught a frightening reflection of herself, trapped beneath the ice. Then she heard clanking sounds from below. Something was caught, trapped beneath her. It was the body of a dark-haired girl under the ice.

Skye ran. She slipped and skidded on the ice, then stumbled to her feet with the ice breaking all around her.

"Help! Help! Somebody help me!" She screamed until her lungs caved. She looked back, but the man had retreated.

She ran.

In the cabin, an old man had just finished his eggs and given his plate to his brown-spotted spaniel dog. As he turned toward the kitchen window, he heard a faint, ghostly cry. He squinted through the fog in the small window over his sink and couldn't believe his eyes.

He took a dishtowel from the counter and rubbed a clear dry circle. *What's a father and daughter doing out on that lake?* He blinked several times.

Then he heard it again, a girl running his way from the middle of the lake, screaming. The man he thought was her father turned back.

"Somethin' fishy, Ladybird," he said to his lone companion. He'd been a widower for a few years now. It had aged him fast, made his skin flaxen and his shoulders slack.

He wore long johns, but he let Ladybird outside. She quickly dusted through the snow to the bank, barking, whirring back and forth, on a guarded circuit.

The sight of the dog heartened Skye, and she ran as fast as she could, her feet soaked and heavy. Then an elderly man stumbled from the cabin door, trying to pull the rest of his boots on.

The hidden current was stronger, and slush formed along the bank. Skye felt shards of ice below her feet. She charged forward, heart hammering in her chest.

The old man ran toward her with his fireplace poker and slid down the bank while Ladybird yelped in the dampened wind.

As Skye dove into the bank, they collided. Her body spilled backward, falling into a few feet of water. He managed to hold out his poker to her, but her numb red hands merely stabbed at it, slipping from any grip. Finally, she clawed at the snowbank until she fell on her stomach safely.

"Is that your father?" He watched the man on the ice running toward the other side until, suddenly, he disappeared into the black water.

"No. No. He's not my dad. He…he took me!"

She turned to face the old man, who watched the abductor's head bob in the water like a hairy sinker.

"It looks like the lake's gonna get him."

Her eyes widened as she pushed her legs through the slush and the snow, falling backward on the bank. The terror in her eyes melted as she watched the bad man struggle for life.

Ladybird came over to Skye and licked her red, swollen face. Her white hat with a little red ball hadn't fallen off, while the rest of her winter clothing had been torn off or ripped to shreds. Her wet socks dripped with icy water.

The old man clutched his chest. He looked ragged, sipping air in shallow breaths.

Skye watched as the bad man in the lake screamed. "Help! Somebody help! I'm gonna die!" A drowning mucous of a man, he attempted to pull himself onto the ice with his arms and elbows. He broke through the ice, getting closer to the shore, only to sink and resurface, looking weaker each time.

The old man wrapped an arm around Skye and pulled her with him. "I've got to get you inside by the fire. You can wrap yourself up in a blanket. I don't want you watchin' this, either."

"Can your dog stay with me, Mister?"

Tears filled his eyes. "Yes. Oh yes, she'll keep you company."

As Skye was ushered toward the door, her tears fell freely as a busted dam. Her body shook uncontrollably as he guided her toward his worn recliner near the fireplace and found his comforter.

"Mister. Sir. Do you…do you have a phone?"

"No, honey, I'm sorry. But I'm gonna get you the police on my CB radio."

She shook beneath the blanket. "I just…I just…I want…to tell my parents I'm safe."

His eyes reddened.

"He can't get me now…can he?"

"You're okay now," he said, choking back tears.

"Okay," she sniffled.

He grabbed his heart pills from the table and found his rifle in the closet by the door, then headed outside. "Don't worry. Just get dry, and then I'll call on the radio."

As the old man stood outside on the bank holding his gun in the air, he fired two shots in the sky. He hoped they would be heard by others searching. He watched the bad man struggle some more, his head barely above water, his arms stabbing at the ice.

"Help!" A weakened and whimpering cry came from the drowning man.

Silence. Suddenly the sound of chopper blades pierced the hazy blue sky. He watched the helicopter fly above the pine trees near the dam.

The helicopter had been dispatched when the girl at the counter from the mini-mart gave the police a description of the unusual man she'd seen and the direction he was heading. The helicopter had been weaving in and out, flying over Route 28. It turned toward the old man waving his arms, but then apparently got a glimpse of a body thrashing in the water.

The helicopter flew down low, creating wind that washed over the drowning soul, blowing shards of ice from him. An inflatable donut was dropped, but he failed to get it around his arms until it stopped dancing long enough to fall over his head. Finally he hooked into it, and they pulled him across the ice.

Before the old man could get back into the cabin and his radio, a patrol car had gotten the call from the helicopter that someone was frantically waving his arms for attention. They were only minutes away. The police car spun near his pile of wood, almost knocking the elderly man off his feet.

"Have you seen a girl?" the one officer yelled, tumbling from the car.

"Yes! Yes!" he screamed, still holding up his rifle.

"Drop your weapon and get down on the ground!"

The officer behind the wheel called for backup while the officer from the passenger side rushed the old man. His pills tumbled into the snow.

"Hands behind your head!"

The old man lifted his head. "She's safe! She's safe!"

The officer put a knee on his neck until he swallowed snow.

"Where is she?" The other officer put a gun to his head.

He could hardly breathe, let alone talk. "In the cabin," he wheezed.

The officer kneed him in the back and grabbed his arms to cuff him.

"You don't understand!" The old man blurted out. The officer shoved his face into the snow until he gasped for air.

His partner bolted through the door, gun drawn on the growling dog.

"No! No!" Skye shouted and ran in front of the gun, wrapped in her blanket. "They saved me! The bad man's on the ice!"

The officer put down his gun. Ladybird bit his finger and lit past him through the open door, tackling the other officer before he could get cuffs on his master.

"He's not the one, Chad! He's not the one! It's the one on the ice!"

They rolled the old man over, but he was pale and could hardly talk. "My pills. I need…my…my pills."

He pointed to the ground, next to Ladybird. The officer who had tried to cuff him got down on his knees and helped him get a capsule under his tongue.

An ambulance and another police car glided past the dam toward the area where they were trying to rescue the drowning man. A man from the helicopter who had lowered the donut watched as it slipped away and the abductor lay on the water's edge.

Meanwhile, an officer wrapped a blanket around the old man. "I'm sorry for what happened, sir. We'll get you to a hospital." He set him down on the stump of a tree.

They all watched the show across the lake to see if the child thief and suspected serial killer would live.

The emergency medical technicians found a footpath through the snow to get to the waterlogged body.

A tall officer with a broad hat and a thick mustache had his gun drawn. It was Tom Brower, the local sheriff who was closest to the case of the first-known abduction, more than a year ago.

The first EMT was a young man built like an ox. He dove into the edge of the water and lifted the man onto the bank. The other EMT, a young woman, was in her rookie year. She had to be the one to take a swing at saving his life, to see if she could pump the water from his chest and force air into his lungs.

Officer Brower yelled at her to hurry. "We need him alive!"

She looked at the fire in the sheriff's eyes, took a deep breath, bent over, and tried to resurrect his precious cargo. She breathed air into the man's lungs and feverishly pushed on his chest, getting a good taste of his molded breath.

Water gushed from his mouth like the eruption of a sewer pipe. The blonde EMT lifted her tangled hair from the face of evil. For her, it would be a memory that not even a stiff drink could wash away.

On the far side of the lake, no one cheered for his life.

Nine
Freeze Warning

S kye Taylor was treated at Utica Memorial Hospital. She had sustained a minor concussion, which meant strict observation by her parents upon being released into their care. She had several scrapes and bruises, but no signs of frostbite.

Whoops of joy filled both sides of the room as the curtain was pulled back. Clutching her parents, Skye kept them both pressed to her face while warm tears fell. She sprang from the cold leather exam table with a wool blanket wrapped around her shoulders. They hugged and kissed, dancing and whirling around the room until her blanket parted in the breeze. Joy unfurled and erupted like a hot geyser.

She couldn't wait to leave, to go home, and to see her baby brother and her grandparents.

First, however, she had to answer a series of questions from the lead investigator, Don Lambert. He had the assistance of an officer named Sheryl Todd, brought in to help him ease the girl's mind after the trauma she had endured. Both officers were in their thirties. Lambert had short-cropped brown hair, with a blue tie and a gray suit. Sheryl, from the Boonville State Police Department, had shoulder-length brunette hair. Her kind hazel eyes found the girl's heart. She quickly let Skye know she had a daughter the same age in school.

The Taylors were allowed to stay, but they watched helplessly from a corner as Skye's memory of events was sifted for clues. She talked about all the things she'd seen and all that she could remember, but since she had escaped before he got her to his den, there wasn't much that revealed new clues to help with the case of Annie Davis, the pastor's missing daughter.

When the detective asked if she had seen any other girls, her eyes froze, trapped in the moment, the horrid memory of what had looked like a girl under the ice. She didn't want to believe it was any more than loose debris, that perhaps the tangled hair was simply a jumble of weeds, nothing more.

But it was something for a new round of searches, something to rekindle the search for Annie. If it turned out that Annie Davis was in that lake, it wouldn't be the kind of answered prayer Reverend Davis and his wife wanted to hear. They prayed for a miracle, the kind that brings a daughter home alive. They didn't pray for closure. For Pastor Davis and his wife, closure was a hammer that smashed your heart to bits.

Mary Davis was the first to see the news flash. A girl kidnapped up north past Forestport had escaped on foot across a thin frozen lake. She called her husband with the news. "Miracle on Snowbird Lake, they're saying."

Why not? She thought. If it wasn't a miracle, then how do you explain it? True, the girl was lighter and faster, and someone would figure the ratio. Someone would do the math and have a scientific explanation for how she stayed above the ice. But it *was* a miracle.

Robert was alone in his office when his wife called. After hanging up, he grabbed his coat and hat and plunged from his church into the cold sun, leaving his phone to ring and reverberate off his sterile office walls. He sped the mile down the street until he slid the car into his driveway.

Misery never loved company more than the two of them together as they offered each other anxious looks and stayed focused on the television for updates. Without a word, they spoke with eyes of torment. The ugliness of their nightmare was catching up to them—they were two people running in place, swallowed by darkness.

The Taylor family had their daughter walking out the door of Utica Memorial, tucked between the two of them. The reporters lay in wait. It's not every day you get a small-town miracle.

They tried to cover her. Joe Taylor lifted his jacket toward her face as the flashbulb cameras plastered her eyes in blinding pain.

"Mr. and Mrs. Taylor, what do you think about the fact that your daughter was cared for at the same hospital as the known abductor?"

Stunned, Joe and Jane Taylor kept walking. They had been told the abductor lived, but until then had no idea he was in the same hospital. The reporters had scored a big surprise. If only they could have gotten a quote. But the Taylors kept moving, sidestepping the roving gang of hyenas who lunged at them while they tried to get into their car.

The pack animals rallied together, snow shifted under their feet, and the clamoring of cameras followed every move before the pounce.

One reporter shoved his microphone into the car as Joe tried to close the crack in his window. This guy had a different approach, a coy diversion from the hard questions. "How's it feel to be a hero, little girl?"

Dumbfounded, she buried herself in her mother's jacket in the backseat. Joe's eyes widened, but his voice was polite. "She's one brave girl who's been through hell. This was the grace of God, pure and simple." They sped away, leaving the starving pack to fight over the morsel.

The child thief's name was Ray Underwood. He was in a coma, on life support, handcuffed and isolated from everyone but a select few hospital staff. His soaked personal belongings were kept under lock and key, waiting for a team of forensic investigators. His shattered and taped glasses remained next to him by the hospital bed. He'd been airlifted to the hospital and placed in an unused wing under construction on the fourth floor. Half a dozen troopers provided tight security.

He was wrapped in a thermal blanket to increase his body temperature and attached to a ventilator. His hands and feet were strapped down. No one but the police, investigators, and a handpicked medical team knew exactly what floor and room he was in. The doctors gave his chance at living as less than 50 percent.

Tom Brower, the sheriff, knew what he had to do. He had to be the one to drive to the Davis home with more empty promises. They had their investigators at the hospital, for what good it would do. He'd already been the bridge between the FBI, the state police, and whoever else had the authority to walk over him. A tall, lanky man, he'd imagined the indented impressions of their heel marks digging in. He was the sheriff of Boonville, for heaven's sake. This was his land, his home, and he knew it better than any one of those spit-and-polish people with pencils in their shirt pockets. The FBI rode in on a white horse surrounded by the state police, but he was the one who had to pick up the pieces and visit the victims in their shattered worlds.

He knocked on their door with the back of his fist. It opened slightly. Robert Davis had been pacing the floor for a few hours, gazing at the television for any more news. Mary opened her mouth at times, but words hardly came out, just more anxiety and deeper lines across her brow. The local television stations were running clipped updates every half-hour or so, and the volume was turned up so loud the sheriff could hardly talk over it.

He put his wide brown hat down in front of his chest and let his mousy brown hair rest on his stiff collar. He swallowed a deep breath and exhaled through his mustache. It gave Mary a chance to turn down the volume on the television while Robert nervously approached him with sad eyes.

Tom stood in the doorway with the remnants of snow dripping down his boots onto the linoleum entry. "No doubt you've heard. I just thought I'd better come over and give you some insight."

Robert extended his hand, but Tom did more—he reached his other arm over and cupped the pastor's shoulder. "We have a good chance to find her now." He let that sink in first. He wanted them to have some hope, something that wouldn't be redefined as a lie.

Mary fingered her disheveled hair with her hands and smoothed her blouse. "I should make a fresh pot of coffee."

"That would be awful nice of you, Mary." The sheriff was on a first-name basis; it meant coffee when he dropped by. Tom Brower didn't go to church much, but when this all went down and he got to know Pastor Robert, he'd started going most Sundays. It was out of compassion for the preacher at first, but lately he went because he needed to be with them. He needed them now. He needed to believe that good could triumph over evil.

And if they were fooling themselves, then he would walk with them in the wilderness until they could go no further. His wife would tell everyone, "That's just how Tom is, he can get all wrapped up in your life as if he might lose his own way home, but he won't quit until he finds the good from it."

They sat down at the kitchen table. Tom politely pulled off his parka and placed it over the back of the seat. When the aroma of coffee widened his nostrils and they could all breathe in its effects, then he could tell Mary he had more on his mind than a few words of encouragement.

Tom observed Robert, who for now kept his emotions in check as if waiting for him to shake the keys of a tortured mind and let the trapped soul out. Mary was trembling as she delivered two steamy cups of coffee to the table. She turned and poured one for herself, and she sat down next to her husband but looked away through the small window above the sink.

She kept her thoughts mundane, easy to keep silent. This room reminded Mary of her childhood, where most conversations grew from the kitchen. When she and her husband bought the house years ago, she had loved the simplicity of its kitchen and the old-fashioned feeling it gave to the rest of the house. Her décor was simple: white painted cabinets and yellow flowered curtains, a kitchen table with red leather chairs. It made the kitchen a place of family discussions, a place where little Rob or Annie could come home from school and eat a snack and lay out their homework, air out their problems of the day, all from a red chair. Rob was in school right now.

Tom licked his mustache, head tilted, searching for the correct words. He looked up and narrowed his eyes in pain. "They figure they know where he kept his victim—or victims, for all we know." He cleared his throat and took another sip. "Thanks for the coffee. I know they say you don't get a cold from the cold, but it sure feels like they're a team."

Robert folded his arms and just looked at his coffee, saying nothing. Mary leaned over the table. "Tom, what have they found? Anything?"

"They're checking out a trailer deep on an abandoned logging road. It looks like he kept some things in it, not much of a place to look at or even spend the night during good weather. Last I was told, it had propane and a working stove, which could easily heat the small place. I don't know much else about it, but so far no evidence that Annie was in it for sure."

The grieving parents looked at each other, unsure if they should breathe a sigh of relief.

"There's more…"

"You mean about Annie?" Robert summoned the courage to look directly at him.

"You know that girl, her name is Skye Taylor…when she crossed the ice, and she swears she saw a body in the water."

Mouth trembling, Mary's voice trailed off with a lost cry. Her face was ashen, and she unleashed a flood of tears. Robert clutched his chest and turned his face down into an invisible pit.

"It could be nothing. Your mind can play tricks when you're running for your own life." Tom's eyes turned red with tears. "You know, people around here can't help think it's a miracle. Might even say so in the paper tomorrow."

Mary turned back toward him and took a labored breath. "Is she all right?"

"Ma'am?"

"The girl."

"She just left the hospital. Believe it or not, the same hospital where they took this man, Ray Underwood."

Robert's eyes widened, then looked boiled, and his neck stiffened.

"I'm glad for her family, and for her. You put the word out, Tom," Mary said. "I want them to know how happy we are for them, and we pray for her recovery. No matter what."

Tom Brower didn't know what to say. His mouth opened but remained void of words. He looked at them both and nodded.

Robert clenched his fists on the table. "What about this guy in the hospital? How sure? I mean…do you think he's the one, the one who took our…our girl?"

"Certain things add up. He parks his car, finds someone alone by the road. His bold way of grabbing a girl during the day." Tom swallowed his own bitter words as he turned his hat in his lap.

Robert took sips of air and looked at his wife as if anxiety were squeezing his stomach, birthing a hard, unforgiving knot.

Tom wanted to finish his words. The air thickened with each one. "They'll do their best to comb the lake with a diver, but the temperatures have been dropping, and the old snow and ice will freeze even harder."

"Ray Underwood, you said?" Robert's voice trailed away from Tom into an invisible chamber of grief.

"He's in a coma, on the fourth floor of the hospital." Tom held nothing back. He told them the chances of recovery were low, and no one wanted Underwood to wake up more than the three of them put together.

Tom stood up. "I've got to go meet with the investigator at the hospital now. I'll tell you what I know when I hear it. You'll always get nothing but the truth. You deserve that much."

Robert sighed and stood to shake his hand. "I know, Tom. Thanks for coming."

"Yes," said Mary. "You didn't have to do this. We appreciate your friend-ship."

The sheriff turned toward the door, fixing his hat to his head.

"Tom," said Robert. "There's a person named, ah…Donna, Donna Brushton. She claims to be a psychic. She came to my office, talked in circles about Annie and then suddenly left."

Tom dropped his head in thought, spinning his hat nervously. "Never heard of her. She a local?"

"She has been now, for some time, but not an old local. I think she stays in those firebrick apartments above Mimi's Diner."

Tom pulled out a pen and pad to write her name down. "Brushton, like that town north, near the Canadian border."

"That's it."

"I'll check this out, probably just an attention seeker. We'll see."

As the sheriff left and cold air from the door shot inside the house, Mary grabbed her husband's arm. Kinetic energy flowed, a surge of relief that warmed them both. Then he realized it was the first time she had reached for him in several months, perhaps longer. The need to have each other's touch had been hidden away in the deep crevasse of their tragedy.

An hour later little Rob Davis bounded through the door from school. His return was a bitter relief, now that they had learned of the day's events on Snowbird Lake. They did their best to manage normalcy in front of him. He smiled at them, and his eyes lit up to see them both home together. They painted on smiles for him and took turns swiping at his hair.

They said nothing in front of him that would trigger alarm, but he noticed that his father deliberately paced in the family room until it seemed he'd wear a trench in the thick wool carpet. Mary took Rob to the side and did her best to muster enough strength to look through his homework, then settled him down in the kitchen with cookies and milk. She was shaking, a tremor that started from her ankles and reached all the way to her shoulders.

Snow swirled outside their home as the sun disappeared behind black clouds in the rolling hills west. Robert's thoughts darkened like the clouds that drifted in with the wind.

He would never tell Tom, but he couldn't stop thinking about how this child thief was tucked away all snug and cozy, with answers he needed about his daughter. Suddenly, a eureka moment grabbed his heart. It flooded his soul and sped through his veins.

He went upstairs to the master bedroom; he had to dig deep into their closet. He found his black outfit, the formal suit with a broad white collar, the one that made him look priestly.

Pastor Davis would go to the hospital, as he had done countless times before. He checked his wallet to be sure he still had the special ministerial card that gave him the privilege of roaming the halls so that he could encourage and pray for those who needed him most. *Perhaps Ray Underwood needs some guidance.*

He went to the mirror and slicked his coal-black hair.

By the time he walked toward the closet to retrieve his long black coat, Mary and Rob were in the family room. Rob was busy setting up his dominoes in a figure eight to create his own cause-and-effect experiment. The

Cartoon Network ran a Tom and Jerry skit. Mary was curled up on the sofa, her eyes closed.

He quietly wrapped the coat around him and walked into the kitchen where he pulled out the butcher knife from the wood block on the counter. He placed it inside his coat. He walked quietly to the door and slowly opened it, letting a cold wind come in.

Mary looked up, startled, rubbing her eyes. "Where ya going?"

"I've got to make a visit for someone who's sick." It was enough truth. He closed the door.

Ten
Black Night Ice

Driving through town, Robert noticed that the nativity in front of the gazebo looked sad. Baby Jesus had been pelted with snow, while mother Mary leaned over in despair. Lighted wreaths adorned the telephone poles as he passed through town. The familiar worn-brick buildings seemed dark and lifeless as he turned down a narrow shortcut toward the city hospital. He didn't have time to save baby Jesus, stuck in the snow. He needed to get to the hospital and find the man—the maggot—who might have stolen his daughter.

He didn't think anyone would notice him at the hospital beyond casual recognition. Doors would open for his clerical collar, presenting an opportunity to slide beneath the legal radar. He didn't know if he would use the knife from the kitchen, but it felt reassuring tucked against his ribcage. He drove with single-minded vision; the snow swirled harmlessly over his windshield like white confetti. For comfort, he traced the outline of the knife with one hand while he kept his other hand steady on the wheel.

Predictions of black ice were in the news nearly as much as the salvation of Skye Taylor from Snowbird Lake and the capture of Ray Underwood. Soon, he would face the child thief; soon, he would look into the face of the one who might have taken his only daughter.

Utica Memorial, a normally bland building the color of parchment, was for now a cheerful setting, trimmed with waves of sparkling icicles in the front entrance and with thick pine wreaths hung above the sliding entry doors.

He pulled into a landscape deceptively innocent on the surface. It was what lay beneath that waited to strike him, like patches of black ice hiding under powdery snow.

The parking lot was adjacent to one of the hospital wings. He reached deep into his pocket and chomped down on the last handful of his Tums.

Turning off the ignition, he waited a moment for the burning sensation in his throat to subside.

Robert stepped from the car, dipping his polished wing-tipped shoes into the unknown. He tugged on the fleece of his collar and felt for the butcher knife in his coat pocket. Suddenly his feet slid out from under him, causing him to fall backward and slam the back of his head on the pavement. He fell so hard that his hands flew into the air and the knife skipped underneath another car.

He saw only the twinkling under his eyelids at first, a smoke-filled haze. He fingered the back of his head while clutching his hat on the icy ground. When he crawled to his knees, he nearly fell again, but managed to gather himself against the car. He felt a throbbing pulse drumming into his head.

Robert took a shallow breath, intending to retrieve the knife until several people came together around the corner of the parking lot, headed toward him. He pulled his hat on, feeling a growing lump. With baby steps, he circumnavigated the broken ridges of snow near the bushes.

The group of people passed by at a safe distance, carefully and quietly walking, seeming to carry a hidden package of their own grief headlong into the threatening wind.

The small of his back grew tight, but he carefully made his way to the entrance. He looked at his hands, thick farmer hands that could squeeze out answers, maybe even snap a windpipe. He wouldn't need the knife after all.

The automatic slider opened, and his mind ignited like an explosive flame to a burner. As he walked past the security guard at the desk, he spied his prize: the elevators.

The security guard, an elderly black man with gray stubble for a beard, motioned him to the center check-in counter. But as soon as the pastor flashed his hospital card, the man just waved him on and looked the other way at more incoming foot traffic.

He was alone as he pushed the yellow button for the fourth floor. He breathed a sigh. Suddenly, a firm hand split the tightening door back open. A clean-shaven state trooper in navy blue, wearing an unzipped parka, wedged himself inside. Robert looked away and pretended to be calm in the trooper's presence as he watched how their warped reflections formed in the stainless steel wall to his right.

The trooper glanced down at the buttons for the floors, but said nothing. He looked straight ahead, waiting for the door to open. His broad shoulders and inflated parka left Robert relegated to a corner. The trooper held tightly to a paper lunch bag and large coffee mug.

Robert stared straight ahead, heart pounding, as if he had gone back in time and was guilty of a schoolhouse prank.

The trooper whistled under his breath. "Number four, huh?"

"Yes, sir," said the pastor.

"Well, you look like a priest. You here to see our boy?"

"I'm his only means of redemption."

"Is that so? What about those things you men call cardinal sins, or whatever?" His mouth twitched.

Robert's mouth opened but nothing came out.

"You know it's restricted? I may have to make a call. I didn't expect this."

The nervous pastor flashed his card and smiled boldly while his stomach knotted with each moment. "I make the rounds here often. The mental health patients are to my right, but if you would be kind enough to let me say a prayer for the man, it might, if nothing else, ease his family's guilt."

The trooper took another moment, scratching his face, before the door opened. "So you're here for a last rite or something?"

"It is a difficult moment, but it needs to be done."

The trooper ran his fingers through tangled brown hair. "I don't see what harm it could do. Even so, we should've gotten confirmation."

"Tom Brower, the county sheriff, goes to my congregation. I talked to him."

"Tom, did you say? He left about an hour ago with the lead investigator." A change rode over the trooper's face. "I would question whether that scum has a soul, but be my guest."

The doors opened and several more troopers appeared, standing and laughing, taking turns telling worn-out jokes.

"Who's your new partner, Steve?" They all turned toward the trooper who stepped with Robert from the elevator.

"Oh, he's all right, just comin' to wave his hand over our scum wonder."

Another trooper, the youngest face of the bunch, studied the cleric and eased off his smile. "I thought they had to be awake and talking to do that sort of thing?"

Steve waved them off. "You're a frickin' heathen, Denny, what would you know?" He motioned for the reverend to follow him down an empty corridor, with a few dimly lit yellow fluorescent lights helping to show the way. "That door. He's the only one on this side; it's mostly under renovation."

From the background, one of the troopers shot back, "Hey, does this mean he's going to heaven?"

One officer sat idly by near the door, his back slumped against the wall and his arms folded, bored out of his mind.

Before the reverend opened the door, he took one last look back to see the uniformed men milling around, some taking seats across from the elevator. In the distance, nurses shuffled down the hall of the mental health wing and one doctor stood alone, staring at his clipboard.

As Robert placed his hand on the door handle, a sour feeling leaked into his stomach, a twisted, ripened churning. His chest cavity filled with emotion; as if bathing in the thick viscosity of oil, his heart worked harder with each moment. He took a labored breath.

He pushed the door silently against the blank wall; it gently closed. He heard the rhythm of pulsating oxygen. A ribbed curtain on wheels remained between the father and the abductor. He took his thumb and forefinger and displaced the curtain. The wheels squeaked.

An echo of Ray Underwood's heart raced across the black monitor in red lines. His mouth was covered with a tube that led to an oxygen pump and tank. Leather straps cut across his body, and underneath, a thermal blanket was tucked in to raise his core body temperature. His eyelids danced the flight of death. His breathing was mechanical, and his body was nearly lifeless. Not much to see, just a sad, pathetic creature edging closer to the extinction of his flesh.

The reverend drew closer, close enough to shift Ray's mask and test his ability to breathe. He wondered if the man could form words with his bloated lips. Underwood looked like something that had slithered up from the primordial soup, some distant cousin to a snake.

Robert had a hard time imagining that a mother could give birth to him, or that a father might come to the hospital claiming him as a precious son.

He found a metal chair and placed his coat over it, his hat on top.

The room had only one set of fluorescent lights burning, and from the curtain, shadows formed toward the corners. A light near the parking lot outside and headlamps from moving cars offered enough of a view between the window and his bed.

Pastor Robert crept toward him and got close enough to spit words in his ear. "Ray, can you hear me? Ray."

He watched the monitor for some sign that his desperate patient was listening.

Ray's dirty blond hair was matted, clinging to his forehead. His eyes flickered under the transient light. "Ray, I need to hear your confession."

The patient's fingers twitched. An IV dripped into his arm.

The reverend bent closer until his lips grazed Ray's ear. He raised his voice. "Ray, can you hear me?"

Underwood's eyelids moved in rapid fire. His body arched against the straps.

"Ray, confess your sins, my son."

The lines on the monitor pulsated more deeply.

The prisoner's eyes opened. His strapped hands squeezed air, and his head jerked. The monitor beeped louder. His eyes trailed Reverend Davis, who stared down at him with hands prepared to squeeze his neck. The cleric's hands shook, electrified in the moment.

"Am I gonna die?" Ray said meekly.

"Yes, I'm afraid so."

Robert held his big hands over Ray Underwood, the same hands that had milked cows with his father, and the same ones that had given thousands of hearty handshakes to his flock. They shook with the desire to squeeze the man's neck until his head exploded.

"Where's Annie?"

Suddenly, the patient's eyes flickered and his body twitched. "She… she loved me, and said so."

A flash like lightning ran across the pastor's eyes. "Tell me where to find her!"

The monitor sounded off an alarm. Ray's body shook violently, his face looked ruptured, and his eyes widened, staring straight at the pastor. His mouth formed a hollow cavern.

His remaining words were lost forever.

Robert grabbed Ray's jaw as if shaping it, to make it work like dough in his hands, to form it into the shape of words that would offer hopeful clues. It appeared Ray Underwood was having a seizure. His body was shutting down.

The door burst open. A doctor and two nurses entered the room with shock equipment ready. The police followed, wrestling with each other through the door.

The nurses watched as the pastor pulled his hands back from Ray's mouth. He looked at them all with a sunken face of ashen disbelief. The police must have sensed his odd behavior.

The two nurses attended to their patient, who was foaming at the mouth.

"Ready! Set. Now!" The hospital team sent a shock through the body of Ray Underwood. Robert stumbled backward, seizing his hat and coat.

Lambert, the lead investigator, stormed in through the room, eyes wide and glaring at the pastor. "Who are you?"

A nurse who lived near Dutch Hollow blurted out, "He's the father of the kidnapped girl!" Everyone looked stunned, as if an anvil had crashed down in the room.

Lambert approached him, sized him up, as if to hold him in the corner.

The doctor gestured angrily. "Everybody leave! We're trying to keep this man alive!"

"He's the father of that missing girl!" the nurse shouted again as they yanked him toward the doorway. Her brown eyes filled with tears.

The doctor gave her a stern look. "That's enough, Liz! I need your help. Keep it together."

Robert was detained on the first floor in a room that looked like a converted broom closet. On this occasion, it was used as a hospital interrogation center.

Tom Brower arrived on the scene to save the day, and with his small-town manner, he persuaded Lambert to let the harmless pastor go home.

With sarcasm that only Lambert himself could have mistaken for wit, the chief investigator asked how the town of Mayberry, where no one was ever truly arrested, could have been relocated so far north.

The sad-faced pastor's shoulders slanted, angled through the vestibule toward the icy landscape.

Tom Brower followed after him. "I got some bad news. Ray Underwood's dead."

Eleven

Hanging Ice

Robert gripped the ice-cold doorknob to his house until it stuck to his hand. He looked up to see a dagger-shaped icicle on the verge of falling, possibly putting an end to his misery. But what of his fractured family behind the door? For months he had felt the jagged edge of his wife's piercing eyes.

And why shouldn't she hate him? After all, he had sent Annie down the road from the church more than a year and a half ago. He was the one who had let her ride her bike alone toward home when she was snatched, kidnapped by the man he'd helped to kill in the hospital. What did that scum take to his grave that could have helped them? His wife blamed him for Annie's disappearance, and the weight of it hung heavier than the two-hundred-pound icicle.

He hesitated beneath the hanging ice, lifting his head and spreading his chest. The fake pine wreath on the door offered little comfort. Reminders abounded everywhere that Christmas was only a few weeks away. He didn't have a Christmas sermon. His heart felt black as coal and lonely as a deep winter well. He was a fake, a faithless cardboard replica of himself.

He eased the door open. A dim light from the den beckoned him as it spread a faint path toward the threshold where he stood. The remaining ground-floor rooms were quiet, lifeless. A sense of relief washed over him to know that his son Rob was sleeping; perhaps Mary had gone to bed as well. He shook off the cold and let his coat and hat fall to the floor.

As he walked toward the back to the den, the coldest room in the house, a bitter wind whistled around the rim of the frosted window. The one bulb in the hallway was enough to see with as he sat down in front of his old oak desk.

He pulled open his front slat drawer and found a scratch pad his daughter had given him with a devotional verse of Scripture for each day. He squinted to read today's verse. It said, "God is love." He found a leaky black pen rolling around. Groping underneath the desk, he located the key to the locked side drawer. Inside was his pistol, smelling of polished steel with a hint of gun oil. After checking the chamber for bullets, he placed it on the center of the desk and paused to think how he should construct the best possible suicide note.

He felt a presence watching him. He jerked his head to find Robbie ducking behind the paneled wall. He quickly placed the gun back where it belonged and left the blank pad and pen behind.

"Rob! Is that you?"

No answer. He heard the shuffling of feet up the stairs and traced the steps above his head to the boy's bed. He felt a hard single tear fall slowly down his cheek. Somehow, after everything, he was human after all. He lived.

Robert discarded his shoes near the entryway and climbed the steps, sliding his hand along the railing, turning the balls of his feet into his warm socks, attempting to feel life again. He breathed deeply, widening his nostrils, scenting his daughter's stack of perfumes from her vacant room across the hall. Her ghostly smells reached inside the tendrils of his soul.

From little Rob's bedroom, a nightlight created a stage from which his father could stand and study his son. Rob pretended to be asleep, so the reverend didn't say a word. He gently tucked the covers around Rob's shoulders and then kissed him on the forehead.

He staggered down the hall drunk on misery, unable to find a balance, tiptoeing to his wife's bedside as if on ice. A faint light stroked the room from the thin shade of their bedroom window. He slipped off his clothes down to his cotton underwear, standing in semidarkness as a sunken pillar of hope.

Was she pretending to be asleep with her face hidden away from him toward the window? He crawled in, but she didn't move a muscle. He wasn't sure if he could get beside her without touching her. He shyly assumed a fetal position and listened intently for her breathing, to sense if she were truly sleeping.

Mary felt his warm breathing on her neckline of thin blonde hairs.

Waves of warm emotion spilled through her body from her spine to her loins. Like a lost cavern, she needed to be explored again. She wanted to let him know she was awake and wanted to be touched. She wanted to feel the heat of his love, to somehow thaw and melt into his arms.

He couldn't remember the last time they'd made love, except that it happened when their bodies accidentally met, and their hormones had raced wild from their self-imposed world of sexual fasting. This had only increased the intensity, like a dam broken free, passionately consuming and carving newfound territory.

He spooned closer, desperate for the affection that eluded him, desperate to find again a true expression of her love. If it could be found, it would be like a deep hidden spring beneath hard rock. Perhaps only they could save each other now. He groped for her and felt her relax to his touch. She groaned as if an old door had opened, spilling the trapped emotions of her tormented existence without the life of their first child.

He wrapped his arms around her until they shared the same heat, the same energy for love, and he felt her resistance ebb. "I'm sorry," he whispered in her ear, until his lips grazed and kissed her lobe.

"All these months, you've thought I don't love you," she said. "I've just stopped living. I see myself deep inside of me, trapped between this life and the next."

"I swear I will find her. I…I wish I could trade my life for Annie's."

"What did the psychic say? Did she tell you something?"

He looked into her red, swollen eyes. He couldn't find the words. Then she turned her back to him.

"Some…some people might think Annie's dead, but God will have his say." Something deep in his heart said he needed to believe it too.

She turned to him. "I'm sorry too." Her lips quivered as she kissed him.

For once, the carnival barker in his dreams did not taunt him to play a game he couldn't win.

Twelve
Echo in the Wilderness

A search-and-recovery team formed in the snow near a natural land bridge used as a launching point for kayaks and canoes during summer months. Snowbird Lake, veiled in white, welcomed them on a finger of land above the water, teasing them with her secrets. A group eased out on the sliver of ice, tethered to safety ropes at shore. They broke open a couple of holes for the divers near where Skye Taylor had seen a dead girl trapped beneath the ice. The divers, in thermal wetsuits, plunged into the murky water and did a cursory search, alarmed that the current might suck them away into thick weeds and twisted debris.

Tom Brower told the Davis family they needed to stay away; they would not be asked to come to the scene unless they were needed to identify something related to their daughter. For once, Robert Davis listened. He figured he had no choice.

Tom drove his Land Rover as far as possible near where Ray Underwood had stuck his car into a snowbank. A tow-truck service had taken the abductor's vehicle to a crime lab in Utica, where the investigator and his team scoured it for clues and let the lab do its forensics. They collected blood samples, fingerprints, and hair follicles.

Tom wore hunting boots with his fur-lined green police parka. He kept his forty-five firmly holstered. As he approached the old trailer, covered with a blue tarp and riddled with shotgun holes, he figured the FBI had done the scope of its examination of the place. Now it was time for him to find the clues they had missed.

The temperature had been steadily dropping to below freezing, and the once-fresh snow had hardened enough so he only sank to his ankles getting there. He opened the thin aluminum door of the small trailer, banging it against the vinyl siding. As he shuffled inside, a field mouse ducked behind a stove, causing him to unhinge his gun. He exhaled through his frosted mustache. Good habitat for mice. Parched and yellowed linoleum curled at the corners, and the smell of wet mildew permeated the confined spaces. He turned over empty cardboard boxes, upended old china saucers and cups, and stepped over empty beer cans and vodka bottles littering the floor.

A deep cold shivered through his bones as he ambled around, perusing the cabinets, pulling out drawers until they crashed to the floor beneath his hands. Mice droppings littered every cavity.

No sign of Annie's belongings was anywhere to be found.

A faint glimmer near a window caught his eye. An oval headlamp sat on a shelf with something colorful inside the rim of the casing that didn't belong. He twisted it with difficulty, red-faced, breathing hard and filling the room with puffs of cold vapor. Finally he got it free, and a pair of small panties fell to the floor.

Tom's eyes widened. He grabbed an old wooden back-scratcher hanging on the wall to his right and lifted the panties into a clear plastic bag from his coat pocket. He left, with that one item, in the cold setting sun.

Days dragged on as snowmobiles swept over the snowbound logging road beyond the trailer. The search in the lake was called off when the weather turned colder. Another snowstorm headed for the mountains, threatening all search parties by land or water.

Robert Davis waited a week; no one called with news of his daughter's case. He trekked out to the places that had been combed, driving his Oldsmobile as far as the plow had made it on the edge of a logging road before turning around. He left his car beneath a canopy of snow-covered pines.

The sun set against thin clouds. He stood out near a culvert where a wedge of the lake slipped in far enough for him to reach it from the road. He flexed his fingers to the sky with his black leather gloves. His long gray coat flapped around his rubber boots as he walked.

A light, thin snow fell against the twilight. Robert stepped toward the opening where divers and the support team had left their now faint impressions on the frozen lake.

Nothing stirred—no wind, nothing but the silent flakes falling, as if he stood in a snow globe, insulated in the wilderness. He was isolated, alone—not even the sounds of coyotes could be heard. He listened for the still small voice of God, but he heard only the sound of emptiness.

The skyline above the lake turned deep rose as the sun disappeared into the western slopes above the pines.

The grieving father walked until he felt sure he stood on the lake itself, spreading his legs apart. He cupped his hands with his gloves and cried, "Annie!"

Something called back, but it was only the echo of his voice reverberating in the white, scarred valley.

"Annie! Annie!" Strangely, it comforted him to hear the sound of her name come back to him in the wilderness, as if he could talk to a broken world. If she was out there, it was his way of letting her know that his love would never end. Love kept him walking through a burning, frozen hell.

The father fell down on his knees in the soft snow. He clutched some of it as if it were confetti and tossed it up in the air until it showered him. Insanity grew inside him, an alien residing in the cradle of his body, waiting to break forward from the shell of existence until a new and darker version of his character was revealed.

"What about you, God? Talk to me. Talk to me." The echo came back with the same words, but lingering, fading into the woods until the reverberation haunted him, making a mockery of his own words.

Robert turned back toward the car, shuffling his legs, thinking about little Skye Taylor and what she knew. If only he could talk to her. He thought about Donna the psychic too, and what the sheriff might have learned about her. And if the devil had met him near the main road, he would have given him a ride, just to learn what he knew. From this time forward, it didn't matter what—or who—tagged along. He just had to get there.

Thirteen
Northern Star

Robert pulled his car up to the Taylor house on a hill, wheels crunching on the snow-packed edge. The night sky cleared until a million stars could be seen. He saw the North Star in all its glory, another reminder that his world was a cold and dim-lit stage.

Pressing the passenger-window button down, he felt warm air escape into the cold gap between himself and the Christmas celebration above. A jigsaw of cars littered the long, sloping driveway. From the laughter that pierced the midnight sky, he figured the party was in full swing, oblivious to his pain as a father without his daughter, without his miracle. He loathed their happiness, and he wondered if Skye Taylor held information that the lead investigator hadn't pressed hard enough for. What if he could show her a picture of his Annie?

He pulled the picture from his shirt pocket, worn and wrinkled, curling on the edges, but still full of color, her hazel eyes complete with wonder. He stepped out from his car and stood in the driveway, wondering if he should go forward. A shiver drove between his shoulder blades and down his spine.

His eyes focused on the opening of light through the picture window. Thick red curtains were half-drawn, festively matching the red pots and green plants on the window ledge inside.

A large Douglas fir was decorated with bunches of silver icicles and a rainbow of flashing bulbs. He saw the angel on top, looking comfortable with arched wings and a horn.

He caught a glimpse of Skye twirling with another child, a smaller child, perhaps a cousin. In that moment, a thought drummed in his heart. Only a few weeks ago, the child thief likely stood where he was standing now. Suddenly he felt cheap, guilty, hung in the gap as if the night air was meant to swallow him whole.

A shadow covered the window. Skye cupped her hands around her eyes and looked at Robert as he stared at her. He imagined that she saw the sad figure of a man standing alone in the road below. Joe Taylor went to the window and looked out, pushing her back, closing the drapes tight.

He jumped into his car with the engine idling. The tail of his coat got stuck in the door, but he drove away under the yellow caution light, listening to the angry shouts of a father as he ran down the driveway chasing him.

Robert turned toward town, spilling more Tums on the floorboard, reaching down for a few until his car nearly skidded off the road.

It was the weekend before Christmas, and he had a sermon to write. He didn't know where to start—until the idea of the North Star got stuck in his head. A sermon was forming in the ashes of his mind like a fire pit rekindled by a cold wind. The embers were dancing in his head as the stars followed him to his church in Dutch Hollow. A shooting star lit up the darkness in front of him, above his circular beams of light, burning up in a flash.

Robert pulled into town and drove as close as he could to the gazebo without getting stuck in the snow. Yanking his coat from the door, he stumbled and fell until his hat rolled on the snow toward the nativity.

Swiping at the snow with both hands, he dug through it toward the nativity scene, aiming to fix the fallen wreck of the eastern pilgrims. First, he saved baby Jesus and cradled him in his arms as if the plastic had life. He gently set him down and turned his attention to poor Mary. She looked sad, tilted, her face nearly eating the snow. He propped her up so she could face the baby. Finally, he looked at Joseph and the shepherd man with his unruly sheep. The men seemed to be looking into outer space, tilted backward. He set them upright, looking toward the baby Jesus.

The bar across the street was shutting down. A group of couples leaving wondered what the lone man was doing next to the gazebo.

"Look, Al!" one of the men shouted as they walked on the sidewalk. They all stopped, the men and women falling into each other.

"Hey, you!" said the other guy with a slur. "Don't be stealing our baby Jesus."

The two girls giggled and laughed, holding each other to keep from falling.

Al pointed his finger toward the pastor. "I ought to come over there and kick your sad-sack butt for Jesus' sake!"

But he fell backward in the snow, and when the other man tried to pick him up, he too lost his legs, doing the splits. The girls roared with laughter all the way up the street and into a nearby house. The men followed in shaky pursuit, leaving the pastor to finish the job of restaging the nativity. Finally, the lowly man of God brushed off the floodlights that illuminated the scene.

From the gazebo, he trudged past his car and entered his church, his cold, dark asylum.

The lights in his office flickered and buzzed, and the oil furnace banged away until heat filled the ancient room. He penned his sermon for Sunday, falling asleep over his desk until the morning light.

Fourteen

Crossing Over Jordan

Deacon Stevens pulled the cord that rang the church bell, his trembling, knotted hands curled by years of arthritis. But the smile on his weathered face reflected the morning sun, a man who lived to ring the bell.

The call rang out beyond the firebrick buildings in town and was heard inside the homes surrounding the main square. The bell vibrated, and snow slithered from the tiled archway of the roof. The elderly deacon held his shaky ground as the bell swayed. Covering his floppy ears with gnarled hands, he ambled down the narrow cherrywood steps. Soon Robert Davis would offer his Christmas sermon, and no one knew what to expect from it.

A snow-hardened circular road outlined the park filled with cars. The Presbyterian church transformed from a cold, dank place, warmed by the parade of people. Parents held children with a stronger grip in a world that had been visited anew by the face of evil. They walked shoulder to shoulder, wearing a maze of multicolored coats, marching inside past the red oak door. They unwound their scarves and folded their coats while keeping their hearts under wraps, heavy with empathy for their pastor.

The sun waxed brilliant outside, coating the snow with a layer of finish.

The sheriff and his wife stepped inside with their two teenage daughters. They took up temporary residence in the back row.

Mary sat dutifully before her husband in the first row with their son. She had her hair pinned in a bun under a royal blue velvet hat. Soft gray-blonde hairs on her neck lifted in the breeze of rustling people. The chatter of voices and the sounds of shuffling feet created an atmosphere of great anticipation. No one seemed disturbed by the hard-backed pews, or the eerie silence that fell when the pastor grabbed the pulpit with his thick hands.

"Today we have a special song," he said with an encouraging smile. "It will be sung by Hailey Parker. She is only twelve years old, but she has a voice that could carry a tune in the wilderness. Foxes and rabbits would halt their busy day and turn to listen when Hailey sings. Even a hibernating bear or two would surface with outstretched paws, enchanted by her sound."

Smiles of anticipation grew from the congregation as Hailey, a small girl with a green dress and thick white stockings, stepped up to the pulpit—but she could hardly see the audience. She gave a confused look to the pastor, who quickly sized up the situation and pulled a stool out from under the pulpit. She nodded with confidence, swiping strands of dark hair from her face.

She looked once to the pianist, who waited with her fingers in the air as if they danced. And then she sang out with boldness: "O holy night, the stars are brightly shining…"

Almost immediately, women dabbed their eyes and men's eyebrows raised with enthusiasm. Hailey electrified the congregation, sending shock waves that ran through each soul. She had no need of a microphone. Her voice even carried across the gazebo, past the nativity scene, and into the ears of a few lonely patrons at the café, dipping stale donuts into hard-boiled coffee. It made people who had never attended a day of church wonder if such an angelic voice had come from heaven itself.

She sang as if she had been born for this moment, and with tender ease, she found the perfect pitch to every note. "…this is the night of the dear Savior's birth."

When she finished, one by one the listeners rose to their feet until finally the whole congregation stood, applauding.

Pastor Davis eased up to the podium while Hailey stepped off the platform into the waiting arms of her beloved parents, sitting directly behind young Rob and his mother. Rob appeared smitten with the girl, and as she passed by him, she offered him a smile.

The choir took over, singing "Hark the Herald Angels Sing" and " O Come All Ye Faithful." Hailey sang along with her parents.

Reverend Davis stood behind the pulpit. A moment of silence, then they prayed together, and old Deacon Stevens led them in a somber but honest voice. As the deacon sat down, all eyes were on the pastor, squeezing the pulpit with his hands.

He cleared his throat. "Some of you dear folks have no doubt wondered about my family, and perhaps you wonder if we have lost our way in the wilderness. If my daughter is with Jesus, then I know she's in a far better place than where we are gathered today." His voice choked for a moment, and his eyes swelled red. "Where is our faith in a broken world filled with evil and darkness? We are not immune from the clutches of evil.

"Where is baby Jesus in all of this? Born in the same world of evil, the same world where King Herod innocently murdered children. Yes, the Christ child was kept safe by the providence of God, and became for us the true king of our hearts for those who will let him reign there." His voice raised an octave higher. "But at what price? Thousands of children under the age of two were slaughtered because King Herod wanted to stop baby Jesus. He feared a challenge to his earthly throne. The evidence of history cannot be denied. There is a catacomb where hundreds, even thousands of baby skeletons lie in a heap of ivory rubble.

"Was the price too much? That is the question we all must answer at some moment in our lives, regardless of where we live—in the small town of Dutch Hollow or in an unknown cave not found on a map. No matter where we live, we still look to the same sky, the same stars, and we all can find the same one that shines the brightest."

His voice became garbled, and he wept in front of his congregation. Some bowed their heads in respect. Some could not look for fear the dam of their emotions would burst.

At the last moment he found his way again. "I have had to answer to God in the midnight hour. My wife and I have discovered what it must have felt like to stand with mothers and fathers who wailed from their thatched rooftops nearly two thousand years ago when Jesus was born, and who asked why. Why their child?

"I looked at the same night sky as you have seen, the same guiding star, and through my tears, I will tell you that if I die this day, the life of Jesus was worth the price of even my own daughter, so long as his light shines brighter. Evil destroys us from without and from within, it carves a gruesome path, it makes us struggle wearily, often in the darkest valleys. But because that evil did not destroy the life of Jesus, with his life we continue. We continue in the valley. We continue on the mountain, and sometimes we move the mountain."

Weeping could be heard from every corner. The pastor's hands trembled as if he would break the pulpit. Tears flowed freely down his face. "Today we have heard the voice of a child. Today the children just like Annie will lead us. They will restore our faith. I am not your leader. I am not worthy. We are all lesser lights reflecting the true light. Together we will walk through the valley of the shadow of death and follow the light."

The sermon ended. No one knew what to do. The pastor walked down the platform, passing everyone on his way to the front door. Deacon Stevens stood, not knowing if he should dismiss the congregation. Little Hailey stood up from the front, all eyes focused on her, and she started singing.

"Silent night, holy night. All is calm, all is bright . . ."

Soon the whole congregation was singing along. When the song ended, they dismissed themselves.

The sheriff and his family took turns hugging the pastor as they emerged from the doorway where he waited. Hailey followed them with a big hug of her own, which reminded Robert of how Annie freely gave her hugs away. As the congregation filed out, he eagerly waited for his wife and son.

His mother came through the door with his brother, visitors for the holiday. She stooped over, took her trembling hand, and cupped his cheek. He held it close and kissed her wrinkles.

He hugged his brother David and told him the door to his house was unlocked; they would be over shortly.

Deacon Stevens walked up and grabbed the pastor's hands fiercely. "Don't leave us, we need you."

At last, Mary and their son walked out of an empty sanctuary.

He hesitated, holding his head down in front of his wife. She walked up to him while Rob made snowballs nearby.

She grasped the lapel of his shirt and breathed into his neck. "I'm pregnant."

Stunned, he looked into the distance, beyond the snow-covered trees, beyond the train tracks in the woods, holding her tightly. He held her as a cushion of soft flesh against the deceptive cold. He stood back to look at her, to see the truth in her sky-blue eyes while firmly pressing her shoulders.

A snowball splattered into his collar, brushing by her face.

Rob had aimed for the wreath on the church door as a target, but his aim had gone awry. His eyes grew wide.

But his father bent down, forging his own snowballs. Poor Robbie had nowhere to hide. His eyes darted, searching for a safe place, when a rapid volley made him fall backward, laughing and shouting. Mary walked down from the steps with a deepening smile.

They left together holding hands, prepared to cross over into the Promised Land. But in his mind, Robert looked back and saw Annie reaching out to be held and carried from the wilderness.

He still needed to find her and bring her home.

Fifteen
January Thaw

Sheriff Brower poured coffee from his silver thermos, inhaling the liquid until it soothed his sore eyes. From his Land Rover, he watched Donna leaving the redbrick apartment building. She clunked down the black iron steps, marching toward the gazebo in the park. Her short, stocky strides were purposeful, gouging a path through the snow. Her lime-green jacket covered half her wrinkled lavender dress, and her black calf boots created a swell of snow that found a naked ring of flesh below the knee. But nothing intimidated her, not even a meeting with the sheriff in the park across from the church where she had once confronted Pastor Davis.

He left the cozy confines of his vehicle, fingering the evidence tucked inside the lining of his parka. Creating his own trail through the snow from the curbside, he bore down on her as she waited for him. The air was heavy. Layers of thick mist rose from the old snow as the temperatures hovered slightly above freezing. A lazy sun hid behind a thin gray veil.

Tom Brower had done a background check on Donna and found that she had lived a nondescript life with her mother in Remsen, a town south of the main highway, until her early thirties. Then she moved into the apartment above Mimi's Diner in town. From a casual discussion Tom had with the landlord, it was obvious that she had moved into her place about the time of Annie's disappearance. Perhaps she intended to follow the case and hoped to offer her assistance at some point. She had no police record and no record of enabling the police within any jurisdiction to solve a case through her purported abilities as a psychic. It was a blank, cold file.

But he did find a bit of old news film in the local library—a newspaper clipping from the early 1970s *Utica Observer Dispatch*.

It showed a black-and-white photo of a teenaged Donna on the front porch of her home, talking to reporters about how she had solved the case of a missing boy who had presumably drowned in a flash flood down the road from them. The nine-year-old boy had gone missing, but it turned out he had been buried in the backyard by his stepfather, who had choked him to death. She claimed that the boy had scared the life out of her when he showed up at the foot of her bed one night, dead and covered in a layer of mud, asking for help.

Apparently the police didn't need her inside information and dismissed her ramblings, because by then the rain had rinsed off part of the boy's hand behind the house. The family's pet collie was seen tugging on the boy, trying to get him out of the washed-up grave. The whole nightmare had unfolded from the mother's kitchen window.

It was never explained what role the self-proclaimed psychic had played in helping to find the boy in the first place, but the mother of the deceased seemed satisfied that Donna had opened up a line of communication between them. A short-lived notoriety followed her.

Tom Brower watched as Donna brushed the snow off the white bench. His eyes finally caught hers, and he stooped under the exposed portal, clutching his jacket as if the evidence inside his lining itched like a wet scar.

"Donna, I'm Tom Brower." He didn't get close enough to reach out his hand, but his tone implied sympathy.

She slid her hands below her jacket, attempting to warm them on her thighs. She waited for him to say more.

"Why wouldn't you come directly to me if you felt you had information about Annie Davis? After all, think about how it feels for the Davis family, for you to offer information out of the blue."

She nodded firmly. "You know, Sheriff, when I was a teen, the police wouldn't talk to me. I've been suffering with this gift for years. I figured if anybody would listen, it would be the father."

He placed his boot on part of the bench next to her. "I'll grant you that, but you should have come to me first." He paused a moment, scratching his mustache. "So why move here?"

"Well, if you must know..." She looked down for a moment, kicking the melting snow with the soles of her feet. "I had a boyfriend."

He lifted his hat and scratched his mousy hair.

"But I mistakenly thought I could help this poor family too. I was tired of living my life in a world of depression with my mother. She's a recluse and would have me hide in my former room for the rest of my life. We all need to find our purpose, don't you agree?"

Tom straightened his hat and then pulled out his evidence bag. The evidence had an official seal on a clear bag; it was easy to see they were panties, a sky-blue color.

He gave them into her outstretched hands. She took them to her bosom and closed her eyes, then handed them back. "I can't help you with those. Don't you have something else?"

His mouth fell, searching for words. Did she know the ones he gave her were only a decoy? He had figured to surprise her with the other evidence bag in his right pocket. He stumbled at the notion that she was ahead of him. He thought about not showing it to her at all. The fact was he'd given her the panties from his daughter's laundry basket at home.

She looked past him.

He pulled the real evidence bag out, the one with the pink panties from the trailer. This time he placed it down next to her on a scratch of snow.

She grasped the bag and closed her eyes, then blinked furiously, crouching over as if stabbed in the chest.

"It's not Annie!" she blurted. "But it's someone else. She hitched north from the thruway toward Old Forge, and he...he gave her a ride."

She handed it back to him, releasing her pain. He searched for the light in her eyes but only saw blackness. "Who? Ray Underwood?"

"It's not Annie. What can I say? I wish I could bring her back, I wish I could stop things from happening. I'm not God! I'm just a lonely woman trying to belong in a world that doesn't want me."

He felt for her plight, a world where she was trapped with a body and mind she didn't want. She was likely reaching out for some attention, and maybe this was the only way she knew how. "Can you tell me anything else about this girl?"

Donna kept silent, head down, dark hair in her face, until he left.

Sixteen
Dead Winter

A uniformed police escort led the black hearse that carried the body of Ray Underwood to the Underwood family farm.

Relatives had worked all night with pick and axe until the frozen black dirt sat like coal tar on a pristine white landscape and a sufficient hole was ready for the coffin. After investigators collected all the evidence, they were satisfied that nothing else needed to be discovered from Underwood's person. His body was shipped in a state-paid limousine, as if it were a funeral procession for a fallen soldier and not a child thief. With good intentions, the authorities wanted him buried away from the public.

On a hillside overlooking the valley near the serpentine Black River and the town of Lowville was the fertile but uneven farm. It was made up of a lopsided old barn and a dilapidated two-story house with a rectangular cupola, sometimes referred to as a widow's walk. It was a place where ancient farmers could walk the perimeter and watch their cows strut for miles. The inherited land under its infamous name stretched for a good many miles beyond rippling creeks, scrub brushes, and skeleton trees.

The land had been in the Underwood name since the early 1800s, and some of the first patriarchs were buried in the family cemetery, including a three-month-old baby girl who supposedly expired from crib death. Ironically, Ray's resting place would be next to the infant's.

The wind was ferocious on the arc of the hill where a curious gathering of cars lined up. It was deep January, and a thin white skin of snow broke and skirted along the road where the news reporters and cameramen stood. Another weathered bunch of people huddled together, standing with placards and reddened faces.

It was an awkward funeral at best. Clyde Underwood, Ray's father, stood outside with his coat flapping in the wind. His thin-cotton hair drew the ice crystals like a magnet. No one else from his house ventured outside;

only curtains moved in the dark background.

Clyde's scorching brown eyes surveyed the police as the limousine driver prepared to step out. Then he eyed the intruders standing on the side of a snow-crusted bank: the media, a few flocks of protesters, and a short brick of a woman standing apart from the others with her head buried in her jacket. He gave a special look of disdain to a couple of elderly women holding placards of protest. One sign said "Baby Killer," written in blood red. The other one said "No justice for Annie."

Robert and Mary sat on the edge of their couch, watching the drama unfold on live television. Robert sprouted deep lines on his forehead, and without blinking watched first to see if he knew the ladies who held their signs in the frigid temperature. Mary sat erect next to her husband. She watched with one hand covering the side of her face as if to deflect the evil procession.

A camera panned in and caught Clyde glaring in the direction of the women.

Clyde Underwood spat a wad of tobacco onto the frozen ground, turning it into brown slurry. "What all these people here for?" he said. "Some kinda show?"

He looked at the closest police officer that could hear him shouting into the wind. But he was no spokesman, just a buttoned-up young patrolman with clean dark gloves, not willing to get dirty with words either.

Clyde wasn't getting anywhere with him, so he flagged an older state policeman who seemed to be in charge. The officer tipped his hat to acknowledge a certain authority. Clyde breathed on him. "Can't ya get these people outta here?"

"No, sir, they have the right to stand on the street edge. They're a good two hundred yards away."

"Let's just get this over with, then," said Clyde. His fingers drummed the smooth pine coffin.

The driver had pulled up to the horse gate, looking at the soupy white-and-black path that spiraled down to the private cemetery. "I'm sure glad I didn't have to try to make that."

Clyde brought his calloused hand down like a sickle. "I don't want anybody else past this."

The father had one camera-shy grown nephew stay and help him anchor the coffin in the back of Clyde's pickup truck. The young man, thin as a rail, was dressed head-to-toe in black. His wife didn't want him there, but when Clyde had showed up at their door, she was afraid not to let her husband go and get it over with. She feared the man as much as she had his son. She confided in a friend, "The demented family lives too close to us."

When Clyde gunned his truck past the gate with the coffin strapped in its bed, the police work was done. News cameras caught the officers wearing evident smiles of relief, as if the ground couldn't swallow Ray Underwood soon enough. As the camera panned the backdrop of people, the pastor, back in his living room, cried out.

"That's her! I see her!"

His shout scared Mary.

"It's her!" He turned to Mary, who struggled to regain her posture.

"What are you talking about?"

"There she is again! Donna Brushton, the woman who claimed to know something about our Annie. She's the one ducking her fat head into her coat like a turtle."

Mary drew closer to the television, watching with her husband as the news team started interviews with those holding signs. "I can't bear to look. See that one? The one that says 'No Justice For Annie.'"

He looked at her. "Do you recognize them?"

She swallowed a lump. "Lord no, nobody from our church."

"But why is that Donna person there?"

"I just want to have a day where my heart doesn't break." No more holding it in, Mary sobbed uncontrollably.

"Thank goodness Rob is still in school." He turned to her with sad eyes and angry tears.

"This nightmare never ends."

"Honey, you're shaking. You need to be careful." He remembered the baby growing inside of her now and attempted to remind her that she was supposed to be on bed rest. She had a few complications and had been ordered to take it easy.

Mary was too heartbroken to be mad her husband's overly protective way. She let it go into that black hole in her mind where everything fell away. She promised herself a new beginning; she convinced herself she could do it. She had to live through harsh realities for the sake of the new baby, and for Robert.

The pastor returned to the television. "Just look at that old guy fighting with his son's casket. He looks like someone who could raise a perverted killer. Did the police really check his house and barn?"

He had lost Mary for the moment. She was drowning in grief, and her eyes looked away.

But when Robert fell back into Mary's arms and leaned his head into her bosom, it was not lost on his ragged mind that this scum pod had a resting place but his daughter did not. Where could Annie lay her head?

He knew he had a rickety bridge back to his family, even if it swayed in the evil winds. He knew that his wife had released him of any blame for losing sight of Annie the day she went missing. But there was one last bridge to hell he needed to take, and it was still out there waiting for him. The devil was calling his name.

Robert didn't see it, but beneath the wrath of heaven that filled the sky with snow, Donna stood as the last person to leave that hill where a mystery waited to be uncovered.

Seventeen

Spring Thaw

cicles melted harmlessly into shallow pools around the sun-splashed corners of the old Taylor house. As Robert climbed from his car below, he could hear rhythmic falling water. Natural rivulets formed in the broken ground, and veins of water trickled down the slope into the roadway. It was an early spring thaw beneath the breast of the mountains. Seduced by the weather and inspired anew to see the miracle girl, the pastor treaded the sloping driveway.

Along the way, he found stubborn patches of ice. As he stepped across the hazards, his rubber shoes felt like clown slippers.

His heart skipped in anticipation as he extended his fisted hand toward the door. As instructed, so as not to wake the baby he left the doorbell alone. The house was quiet and dark, while sunlight stretched and reflected on remnants of snow in the yard. When he knocked, it sounded to him like the *clop-clop* of horses' hooves. He heard feet scampering for the door.

As the door inched open, Skye Taylor looked up at him with her bright blue eyes. Joe Taylor draped his long arms around her shoulders. Abby, the golden Labrador, sniffed the visitor's rubber boots and poked her nose under his vanilla trench coat.

Robert stooped down and smiled at Skye. "So you're the one we heard so much about?" He cupped her hand as if she were a princess.

She blushed through freckles and crinkled her nose. The dog slurped at the pastor's face. When he stood up, Joe Taylor offered a stiff handshake. "Sorry, our dog is jealous over all the attention our daughter gets."

"I don't mean to add more to your burden."

Joe, with his blue eyes rimmed in gray, couldn't hide his concern. "No. No apology. You're welcome here. Can I take your coat?"

Pastor Davis shook off his coat and studied the slush at his feet.

Joe smiled. "Please. Come into our living room."

Robert slipped off his rubber shoes and followed Skye and the dog toward the spacious room. He remembered that there had been a large Christmas tree here, visible from the road.

He and the girl sat down on the sofa nearest the fireplace filled with old ashes. He sank snugly into the cushions. Skye sat a few feet away from him, her feet dangling above the floor. Abby instantly nestled beneath her stocking feet, creating a soft footstool.

Joe sat in a crimson chair with weathered arms. He leaned forward, sitting on the edge, seemingly searching for words of comfort.

The pastor was drained, his heart thawing and pooling into an unknown stream. He fidgeted on the sofa, enamored by Skye's adventurous blue eyes. It was obvious to him that she had kept her innocence. If the dead kidnapper had taken anything from her, it didn't show in her eyes. He felt certain that God was working something out between his loss and her miracle. Skye was teaching him without words. Liquid warmth radiated through his spine as he sank further into the couch, heaving a deep sigh.

Joe turned his head. "Can I get you a cup of coffee?"

"No, thanks," the pastor said. "I emptied a pot in my office this morning."

The girl stretched her legs, attempting to rub the dog's back with the balls of her feet.

Silence drifted between them.

"I hope I didn't wake your precious little boy from his nap."

"Oh, my wife went upstairs to his room to check on him. I'm sure he's sleeping soundly."

"Earlier, on the phone, I didn't share with you the news of my wife," said the pastor.

Skye perked up to listen.

"She's due to have our third child by early September."

"Really?" said the girl.

"You know, Skye, you have the prettiest name for a girl I have ever heard. When I say it, I think of a blue sky full of promise."

She blushed.

Joe spoke. "We can't take credit for that. Her first parents were from Oklahoma and must have been inspired by the avalanche of Indian names in that country."

"You are blessed, Skye, to have such wonderful parents now who love you so much. And then the icing on the cake is your little brother."

She smiled unashamedly and inched closer to Robert. "I'd like to come see your new baby someday."

"Yes. Perhaps when we have a dedication you can be there for it?" Then he thought about when Annie was dedicated as a baby, and he momentarily lost his smile.

Robert gently reached inside his sweater to his shirt pocket, where he faithfully kept his tattered picture of Annie. He pulled it out and let her have a good look at it.

Joe looked nervous, and Skye's eyes widened. "She's so pretty. How old was...was she in this picture?"

"She was eleven, and until I find her, she will always be eleven." He felt tears begin to well in his eyes.

Robert Davis set the picture down on the coffee table. Joe pulled his reading glasses from his shirt pocket and swiped a bead of sweat from his forehead. "She's beautiful. She favors you, no offense to your wife."

"None taken. My boy and daughter have tended to favor me with their looks, the poor kids. I'm sorry they bear that burden. However, you should see the way they carry themselves with a spitfire purpose. Just like their mother."

Another wave of silence crossed over the room. The pastor continued. "When I was a boy, my grandparents had a camp near the St. Lawrence River. I was a good swimmer at fourteen, but more stupid than brave. I went too far and the current had me. I panicked and began to drown . . ."

Joe and Skye sat in rapt attention as the story unfolded. Meanwhile, Jane crept down the stairs and sat on the bottom edge, just out of view. The pastor felt her presence and caught her listening shadow.

"It was like slow-motion death. I felt like a sinker in the current, and the shore seemed to be getting further away. Both my grandparents must have stepped inside. I gulped some water. And if you know anything about the river, even though it was mid-July, the water was ice cold."

Skye leaned next to him and listened to the story unfold.

Robert's brown eyes glistened as he finished the story. "Suddenly I realized what my grandpa had told me. 'If the current gets you, don't swim directly into it but take sidestrokes, relax, and let your body drift a bit.' I was scared for sure. Afraid I would die. But I did the unnatural thing. I let this invisible current take me. Finally I pulled up along a shallow part and inched my way toward a neighbor's backyard."

"Did they find you?" she asked.

"I walked home and never told them." His eyes swelled with tears. "Lately, I think God is like that current that gets the best of us. He's still in control, all right. And we look for him, but we don't see him during that moment of panic. Then we have two choices. We can fight the current and lose, or we can trust where it will lead—and it's scary because it takes us to an unfamiliar shore. Skye, it really doesn't matter if you can't tell me more about my Annie. I think I needed this moment so I could see the miracle in you. I think like most people, my miracle is found in God's secret current. He's taking me to another shore, and somehow I know Annie will be there."

"I think I understand." Unashamedly, Skye blinked large tears. She turned and hugged him firmly, and it ran through him like a bolt of electricity.

The two men stood up together, wiping away tears. Jane came from around the corner. "Thanks, Reverend." She, too, had tears that were not so easy to hide.

"Ma'am, please call me pastor. I've never liked reverend. When I leave here I walk with feet of clay, just a man. I don't think I can live up to 'reverend' status."

She awkwardly hugged him and wiped the tears from her eyes. "I thank you," she said, "because her father and I know the guilt she's carried all these months. When Skye found out about your daughter and what happened, she felt like she'd let you down."

"It's okay. I believe God knew we needed each other." He pinched the tears from his eyes and turned to the miracle girl. "You have given me new strength. I'm blessed to know you. Proudly wear that miracle, just like a rose in the winter."

On his way to the door, Abby waved her tail for attention. He sank down and massaged her ears. "We should all get together on a warm sunny day, with nothing but the blue sky."

"I'd like that." Skye tugged on his coat as he was about to step from the door. "I don't know if I can explain it, but I really think she was with me when I ran across the ice. It was like she was talking in my head, telling me to run, not to look back."

"I believe you, honey. Thanks."

"Mr. Pastor, wait!" She ran into the chilly air. "There's more. Once I had a dream. She was standing on the other shore calling me. She took my hand to safety, and she played with me in the snow. When I asked her why she didn't want to make a snow angeal, she said, 'Because I am an angeal.'" Tears filled her eyes. "Maybe that means something?"

He looked to her parents, who nodded their approval. He took his fingers and brushed them across her wet ivory cheeks. "It means *God's messenger.*"

He quickly turned away and stumbled down the driveway, tears streaming down his face.

Eighteen

A Midnight Run

Late one evening, Robert Davis sat alone in his office. He traced with his index finger the initial his daughter had carved on the oak desk. He caressed the rising slant of the A and the half-moon circle of the D, unbroken. A red-hot carving knife had left the same scar in his heart.

With his desk cleared of all his books, he hugged her memory. He rested his face down on the cold, smooth surface with one eye open, remembering the sturdiness of her lines, cherishing her personality, a girl who knew how to work against the grain. As he looked over the desk and breathed in the smell of old wood, with the corner of his eye he found the darkened doorway to a lifeless sanctuary.

His eyes ripened with tears, and he thought about how Donna had come into his office months ago. Perhaps she had found traces of his daughter in his office. Would it be enough to color in a picture and find his Annie?

For months he had resisted calling on her, as if it revealed a weakness in him. Sheriff Brower had called and told him she had nothing significant to offer. "She's a lonely misfit in this world, likely seeking attention," he had said. But he couldn't shake off how she had moved into one of those old second-story apartments above the village shops and Mimi's Diner, across the park from his church. Why there? Had she been watching him?

He took no thought to grab his jacket. He dashed through the darkness down the corridor to the main door. An invisible current swept through him, beneath broken clouds of endless stars. He wasn't about to let himself drown in sorrow any longer.

He walked briskly beneath the budding trees of spring in the midnight chill. Floodlights from the gazebo marked his trail. He skirted across worn swaths of weathered grass while his feet kicked the loose pebbles of stone on the horseshoe road outlining the park.

He stopped in the pitch darkness underneath the iron steps of the fire escape. Widening his nostrils and sucking air, he could taste the cold sweat of molded brick. His feet smacked down on each step like heavy mallets.

On the landing, he recalled the number the sheriff had given him on the phone. The number six. How could a cleric forget that?

With tremendous, blinding force from his shoulder, he shoved the metal side door open. Eyes darting, head spinning, he stumbled down the dim-lit hall. He tripped into a pile of assorted boxes filled with papers and clothing. The corridor reeked of leaky metal pipes, and the mucus-colored carpet smelled of dead mice.

The number six was slanted, with only one nail holding it in place.

He heard the faint sound of music playing from a stereo. When his hand trembled upward to knock, a cold draft inched the door open.

He saw an outline of her raven hair and head anchored in a large chair, obscuring her remaining features. A scant light filtered from Main Street through a picture window with a thick, half-drawn curtain.

Tilting his head further inside, he called into her dark world like a schoolboy late for his tutor. "Donna."

With the back of his hand to the door, it swung open further. "Donna. It's Pastor Davis. You okay?"

No answer, just a high-pitched screeching from the radio—songs from the seventies.

The door half-open, he took baby steps toward the large open room filled with the shadows of scattered belongings. He could see the red button eyes of the gleaming radio above piles of debris stacked on the kitchen table. A new song started playing. "The Lion Sleeps Tonight." The falsetto sounds of the classic lofted into the ashen room.

He half-expected that she was baiting him to draw closer, as if she had eyes, veiled eyes, in the back of her head. It made him more determined. After all, she had invaded his life but never given him one good thing to work with in order to find Annie. Maybe, after all, it was just a bunch of spooky bull. The other half of him expected her head to turn, like the child in *The Exorcist*. But he was prepared to laugh before the devil did. Nothing would stop him from confronting her now.

He touched her shoulder with a tip of his finger. She didn't flinch.

The draft followed him in and stirred up an acrid smell that stung his nostrils. He looked down into the pale glimmer of light over her chair. Arms hung down, slacked in defeat. Fingers dipped into a dark puddle. He shook her shoulder, and her head slumped.

She was dead.

He turned to run and slipped in a pool of blood. His body slammed backward, and he cracked his head on the hardwood floor. Then he saw the razor blade that had dropped from her hand: shiny silver metal pasted in blood. A notebook slipped from her lap into the crimson.

He crawled to his knees, his heart hammering in his ears. He stood, trembling with acidic fear. Turning his head sideways, he worked up enough courage to bring his finger to her neck and feel for a pulse. He tilted her head back. The folds of her neck felt like hard rubber. No pulse. Her dark eyes, empty like black marbles, searched nothing.

He felt cold sweat rise from his neck. Eyes darting in fear, they pinged to the window overlooking an empty street and then back toward the faint opening of the doorway. He looked down once more to his feet and grabbed what now appeared to be a sketchbook doused with her blood. He tucked it into his belt loop and fumbled for the door.

In the background, the song played on. "In the jungle, the mighty jungle, the lion sleeps tonight. In the jungle, the quiet jungle, the lion sleeps tonight…"

He retreated to the door, clicking it shut. From the light of the hallway he could see his white shirt smeared with blood. Like a man on fire, he ran. Bursting through the escape door, clambering down the steel grate, he raced across the dewy ground until he reached the inner sanctum of his church.

He knew he had to call the sheriff, but he couldn't be seen as a bloody mess.

Nineteen
A Tale of Blood

Pastor Davis rinsed his bloody white shirt in the bathroom sink next to his office. Then, while soaking it in soapy water, he took a clean, pressed shirt from behind the door. He buttoned up, searching in the mirror for the man he remembered himself to be. A sliver of blood stained the ridge of his nose. He wetted a hand towel and dabbed at it, then placed the towel on the back of his sore head for a moment. He looked into the mirror again, wondering what a schizophrenic is supposed to look like. The lines in his forehead etched deeper.

Only minutes had passed when he sank into his office chair and breathed a deep sigh. He knew he had to make the phone call to Sheriff Brower. He had to get him moving in the right direction quickly, to see the apartment and know that it was obvious that Donna had taken her own life.

He sat down with Donna's bloody sketchbook in front of him, tempted to leaf through it. After shoving it into his top drawer, he started pushing buttons on his black phone, a number he had memorized. He looked at the clock, the one on the wall of faith next to an entire cast of grim clerics who had laid this foundation before him. His headache pounded while the clock ticked like a hammer. It was half an hour past midnight.

He heard the sheriff's muffled voice on the second ring. "Hello, who is this?"

His wife was in the background. "What...what is it?"

"Tom, I found something awful. I walked over to Donna's place across the park..."

The sheriff recognized his voice. "You what?"

"I went to see her. There was no answer. The door was open a crack, and I called out. She was near the window in a chair. I knew something was wrong..."

"You walked in?"

"She's dead, Tom. I think she killed herself."

"What? You think or you know she's dead?"

"I'm sure."

"Are you there now?"

"Where?"

"In the apartment, on her phone."

"I'm in my church office now."

"Oh, crap! I'm calling the ambulance. They'll be there in a few minutes. Just stay put till I see you. Wait. Don't hang up. Did you disturb anything?"

Tears boiled in the pastor's eyes. "Oh boy…did I! Tom, it was dark, I was concerned, and I slipped on her blood. I checked for a pulse and then left."

Silence, and then a sigh filled the vacuum between them.

"Stay where you are. I'm sure it happened the way you said. I'll get a report from you with my deputy."

Robert hung up the phone and took a deep breath. He opened the drawer and thumbed through the pages of the sketchbook: sometimes notes, sometimes pictures of stick men and women, sketches of various scenes, even a faint drawing of an old house in the middle of a forest. A package of Tums rolled forward. He put a stack of them in his mouth and chomped down.

Several moments passed, and then a beacon of colored lights from the ambulance pulsated across his window. He flipped on the switch to the sanctuary from the wall near his office and looked at his shoes. No blood; the grass must have wiped them clean.

He paced up and down the hardwood floor with a *click clack* back and forth, sometimes sliding his hand along the smooth wooden pews. He mused about the sketchbook; he should hand it over to Tom. He had done most everything correctly, but he shouldn't have run like that. A paranoid moment had struck him when he imagined that someone from another apartment might see the stalwart pastor in a blood-soaked shirt. But who could blame him? He rode on everyone's sympathy as if he owned a pure white horse.

He fell back into his chair and spied a spot of blood. He took a tissue and spat, wiping the stain from his desk.

The sheriff stood in the doorway to his office, leaning his lanky body against it. He shook his head, biting the overhang of his mustache and folding his arms.

Pastor Davis clenched the tissue in his hand as Tom drew closer. A thought plunged into his heart that he should give up the notepad before things went too far. What if the last thing she'd written was a suicide note?

The sheriff pressed forward. "She was one messed-up gal. It was pretty obvious she cut her arms open—not across like an amateur, straight down like a pro." The sheriff used his hands in a sweeping motion down his arm to show what it might have looked like. He pushed his hat above his forehead and then placed it on the pastor's coatrack.

"Hey, Tom." Kyle Foster, his young officer, twirled his hat in the archway. He had energetic eyes and a round, boyish face. His hair was short-cropped and sandy brown. "They put her in a body bag and they're transporting her in the ambulance. We're just waiting for the investigator to come up from Utica and have a look around."

Tom walked over to the pastor and put both hands on his shoulders. "Don't worry about anything. You gave me an accurate statement."

The pastor felt childlike, as if caught cheating on a test. He turned to Tom. "Are you sure?"

"The investigator will get our report of your eventful night, and that should sum it up for him. It's obvious she killed herself, and if they dig up anything unusual, he might get back to you. How's that sound?"

"Okay, I guess."

"Not unless you think I should look in your front desk for a visa to another country?" Tom squeezed his shoulders. "You know, that's a pretty good-sized lump on your head. We should have one of the paramedics come and check it out."

"It's okay. I just need to get to the house and soak for a while."

"Not a bad idea."

Tom took his John Wayne stroll toward the doorway, retrieving his hat, and then turned back. "Oh, and by the way, let me handle things from here on out. It's impossible for me to know how you feel, but you could get seriously hurt. Think of your family, my friend, and that precious baby on the way."

"I know, but what does a father do after he lets his daughter leave on a bike and then gets a call from his wife saying she never made it home? I was the one who held her last. When we find her, I need to hold her first. I need to tell her I'm sorry. I need her forgiveness." He sobbed once into his hands.

The sheriff didn't know what to say. He turned his head toward his deputy, and his words got choked. He cleared his throat and started over. "Most of the heavy snows have melted, and…and the lake ice is gone, but we need to go deeper into the forest too. We need to turn over every stump and every rock."

"Thanks for being a good friend, Tom."

With tears in his eyes, the sheriff tipped his hat in the doorway as he and the deputy gave Robert Davis back his lonely world.

Twenty
Acid Rain

Passing out on the couch, Robert was catapulted into a world of rambling dreams. One particular scene stretched the fabric of his mind.

He was cutting a path through a veil of snow across a thin, frozen lake. Unbridled, he raced for the sound of his daughter's voice across the shore. He fell without warning. Thrashing, unable to climb over shards of ice, he sank into a watery grave. And that's when he saw her. Her dead eyes blinked open in the ice-cold water, and her hair floated around her head.

Submerged in his nightmare, he rallied, awakening in a cold sweat only to fall back, further sinking into a disturbed state of dreams.

He had explained all the prior events to Mary: the unexpected discovery of Donna's dead body, slipping on her blood, and the meeting with the sheriff. He shared everything with her in that dark hour except for the sketchbook tucked under the cushion of the couch. He insisted his wife get her sleep, resting like she was supposed to, protecting the new life swelling inside her.

Before sleep seized him, he studied each sketch for answers. One by one he flipped through them until he felt the acid churning in his stomach. A maddening rage took him, claws raking the lining of his stomach. He boiled, glaring at the last page. A sketch of the Underwood family graveyard was complete with mounds, tombs, and names. One such name: Annie Davis. She was shown in the grave next to her accused abductor Ray Underwood, as if they were meant to be together.

Was it possible? Could Annie be buried under everyone's noses where a baby had been buried generations ago? Did Ray Underwood put her there before he died? Was this the psychic's final message?

Other pages had lost their significance. The forest of trees, cabin, trailer, and lake—it seemed as if the sketches had been kept like a log, a timeline of events that Donna might have followed. But nothing possessed his mind like the one drawing of the graveyard. The image dug deep into his subconscious and was dredged up along with all the other fragments littered there.

Finally, the last strands of sleep were severed.

At four in the morning, he numbly laced his boots, threw on his rain jacket, and headed into the garage. He found his pickaxe and pointed shovel, placing them in the trunk of his car.

A cold drizzle fell to the ground, like acid rain bleaching the landscape. As he started his car, the lights did little to break the ashen mist.

He gripped the wheel, and his thoughts turned like the final blank scenes on a projector, spinning, slapping away at emptiness.

At four-thirty in the morning, he arrived on the knoll of the hill where the Underwood farm had a grand view of the valley below. In the dead of night, darkness prevailed—so dark the mist appeared luminous. With his glimpse of the family cemetery, Robert's focus was shortsighted to the point of frothing madness.

There was a path beside the scab-gray barn on the hill furthest from the house. It was a narrow strip of tractor grooves along a broken barbed-wire fence.

Finding the old horse gate, he stood outside, pushing on it until it shuddered open. He jumped in his car and searched for any lights piercing the mist from the farmhouse. Splashing through deep puddles, he navigated the uneven lane.

Snaking to a stop near the muck and mud, he swerved near the old oak tree where the ground was settled and elevated enough to turn around.

He grabbed his flashlight from the glove box and aimed it toward the row of marked graves. Tilted and bleached stone slabs with engraved names and dates were weathered beyond distinction. Ray Underwood's plot had no marker, only slat-wood sticks wired together in a haphazard cross.

He bent over and wiped the cow dirt from the stone marker next to the killer. An infant's name—Emma Underwood, born 1889—but no date of her death, just *Died at two months.*

This is it, the pastor said to God. *After this, I'm done.* He fell to his knees, and the flashlight dropped to the ground. "I'm done, God!" he called into the hoary night. "If she's not here, then you don't want me to find her. You can have her. I give up. She's all yours!"

He took shallow breaths and worked the pickaxe, jamming it into the soft ground between sobs. The sandy gravel broke like warm cake. He went to the car and grabbed his shovel from the trunk. He made good progress while the mist thinned and vanished into the sky like rising ghosts.

He checked his watch; it was near five in the morning. Darkness was his shield. He still had enough time, and then he could hold to his resolution with God. He could go home and trace the form of the new baby growing inside his wife. He could start over with his eleven-year-old son. He could still save what was left of his family. God had planted a few seeds of grace.

With every lunge and kick of his foot to the heel of the shovel, he felt that he was on the verge of an answer. At any moment he thought to hear the hollowed tap of pinewood beneath his feet.

A dim sliver of daybreak slipped through the horizon, and then it happened. The shovel cracked into old wood, soft, like corkboard.

In the distance, on the hill by the barn, his eye caught high beams drifting toward him in waves.

He jumped into the hole and gripped the coffin. With one great thrust he unhinged it. Then the lights from the pickup stabbed his eyes.

Twenty-One
Hail Fire Rain

ey! Hey! What the…!"

A shotgun lifted from the headlights toward his chest.

Robert Davis shut his eyes and bowed his head in the grave, listening for death, but the blast never came.

Clyde Underwood stood on his son's grave, red-faced, spit blowing from his mouth. "Who are you?"

The pastor, wild-eyed like a raccoon, mumbled chafed, incoherent words with a laboring breath. He raised his trembling hands over his head and looked down at the small coffin.

The angry man jabbed the shotgun toward him. "An infant's in that coffin. You robbin' a grave?"

"No! No!" He grabbed his head and hunched his shoulders.

Clyde kept the shotgun aimed at his chest. "I can care a whole lot less than you think. You a private investigator?"

Licking his chapped lips and wetting his dry tongue, he choked out the words. "I'm…I'm looking for my daughter."

Clyde stumbled backward. A menacing sky stirred above them. "I seen you. I seen you on the news. Holy night turned day!" He eased the shotgun to his side, kneeling down and scratching his knotted forehead. "You're the preacher who's been lookin' for his daughter."

A stiff blank stare went past Clyde.

Clyde rubbed his face. "You wanna know if she's in that box? Have you lost your freakin' mind?"

Reaching up in the pile of dirt for his flashlight, the pastor shined it into the box. There was a pile of small, slender bones, some no bigger than a wishbone.

"Look what you done! You got some death wish? I coulda blown your head off."

Robert knelt down by the broken coffin, weeping. "I'm sorry. I'm sorry. I thought she was here."

He hadn't known what he might find, perhaps her clothing or a piece of fabric that could have been identified. Something of Annie should have been there. But then, deep inside, a pinhole of hope pricked open his mind.

"Look, I don't want you here," said Clyde. "I don't want no more news or police. Just leave my family alone." He offered Robert the barrel of his gun to pull himself up.

Suddenly, the sky released a torrent of hail-fire pellets. It was the kind of hail that leaves welts on exposed flesh. The morning sun was a shadowy circle in the distance.

The pastor raised his voice above the drumming on the vehicles. "Please, can you help me find her?"

They stood there, no hats, no jackets, just letting the ice sting and melt over them.

Clyde gave him a hard, long look. "I'll tell you what I know. But you have to follow me up the path and meet me in the barn. Now!" He pointed a finger at his car. "Do it before this piece of crap Oldsmobile can't make the knoll."

The pastor swerved his way behind Underwood until his tires were thick with mud, but he made it past the gate. He figured this would be okay. The man didn't want any more publicity. But suddenly the realization struck him that no one knew where he was. It made for a dangerous opportunity with someone who also didn't want to be seen. That's when his beeper went off; his wife was calling. But he couldn't tell her anything. Not yet.

Robert forgot about the sketchbook. It sat next to the beeper in the front seat while he focused on Clyde, who was walking through the mud puddles in his knee-high black boots, disappearing into the barn with his shotgun.

As he dove out from his car under heaven's volley, he wondered just how far this hell would go. Was this all one seamless dream from earlier?

The barn, just an ashen scab on a hill, had no paint, no real color. It was tilted, ready to fall over in the next gust of wind. Robert pulled the slat door back and stepped inside.

Chickens clucked in the loft, and there was an old gray mare in the corner. The smell of damp hay widened the pastor's nostrils. A couple of hay bales lay near the snorting horse. Clyde was nowhere to be seen, but Robert could hear him rustling behind a half-wall of rusty tools.

Clyde came from around a workbench with a picture. He walked over and showed it to the pastor, who reached for it with shaking hands. A fluorescent light from the workbench gave him the only good angle to see it.

"These are my other two boys," he said. "They got burned pretty badly."

Robert noticed that the boys glumly stared away from the camera. One had his hands bent, elbows out. Burns were etched across his skin, one on his neck, the other on his face and arms.

"That's what my oldest son did to my boys. They're retarded. He tortured 'em worse than a cat. The wife and me, we thought we could trust him to babysit. He played this game. Here in the barn, at that pole. He tied 'em both up and poured a circle of gasoline around 'em. He'd light a match, and they'd have to blow it out before it fell on the hay. It's a wonder the barn didn't burn down. He put the fire out, but not before the boys was badly burned."

Clyde looked at the pastor, his head tilted, his wet cotton hair twisted. His somber blue eyes looked at Robert for a moment as if he expected some profound theological answer amid the damp stench of the barn. Robert didn't know what to say. His head throbbed, his body ached, and it felt to him as if the walls of the barn were closing in. He bent down over a hay bale as if to pray, but he was trying to keep from passing out.

"My oldest boy was one sick son of a gun, you think I wanted this? You think I made him that way, don't ya? I shoulda killed him and put *him* in that grave."

"In some ways it makes us both the same."

Clyde's eyes widened with a look of disbelief. He dug for his tongue. "How's that, Rev?"

"We both feel some responsibility for what happened to our children. That maybe we could have prevented things. Perhaps this moment was, after all, no accident."

Clyde looked up toward the loft in a scoffing manner. "So maybe I tell you what I know. I tell you what the police don't ask. Because with me and them, if they don't ask, I don't tell."

Robert, sitting on the hay bale, leaned forward and ran his fingers through his wet hair, listening.

The old man walked over to him with another picture from the workbench. This one showed a pine-green cabin with black shingles. Below it was a creek, the same creek that filtered into Snowbird Lake.

"No one knows about this place," he said. "It was built on state land. So in theory it don't exist. And I never told you neither. You send someone here; I'll have you up on charges. You leave me alone. Just try and see if she's there. But don't ever come back here again, or then I care a lot less than you know. Got it?"

"Where?" He sat there with the picture, like it would melt in his hands, staring at Underwood as if he had pointed to one of a billion needles in a haystack.

"Wake up, man!" Angrily he raised his fist into the damp air. "They never got that far. They thought he used a broke-down trailer all the while. The police figured at the end of the logging road they checked every trailer, every shed and outhouse along the creek. But it's hidden on state land! No one could have found it in the deep snow until now."

Robert found his legs and turned to walk away. He couldn't look at Clyde anymore and imagine the wasteland of genetic misfires.

"I have a daughter too, what's left of her. And she don't talk no more."

The pastor shivered, wondering what evil had been done to her.

Armed with his picture and the knowledge to go where the logging road ended, he escaped through the doorway. But he could hear Clyde shouting.

"Mother Nature, she kept you down pretty good there, Reverend, she kept you in her grip, but now she'll give you a chance and let you go!"

Twenty-Two
Mudslide

At the Sunshine Mini-Mart in Lowville, Robert Davis stopped to use the pay phone and call his wife. His trembling fingers pressed the silver buttons. An Amish cart passed by, its horse stamping on the rain-soaked pavement. A little boy, tucked between his parents and wearing a thin round hat like his father's, appeared sheltered from the cares of this world—as if time granted favors. The pastor looked down and thumbed the mud from his watch. It was nearly seven in the morning.

Mary answered the phone on the first ring.

"Don't say anything. Please hear me out. I'm going to find Annie. This time, I think I know where she is."

A deep sigh, then a gulf of silence rose between them.

Muffled cries crackled through the receiver to his ear. "Alive," she said. "Tell me she's alive." He heard stifling sobs.

"You know my heart will always say yes, but no matter what I find, I won't let that scum of a bastard destroy the rest of our lives, or what's left of us."

"I can't even hold what's left?"

Silence.

"Will it finally end today?" she asked. Her voice trembled.

"Soon. I think, very soon."

"You're alone? Don't do this without Tom."

"Call him. He can start down the logging road near that trailer where they found evidence, and then tell him to keep going until they find my car near a footpath. There's a house hidden on state land."

"Wait," she said. "Wait for Tom. He cares about us. Give him a chance. Why are you doing this alone? We need you. Your son needs you. If not for me, do it for him. Just don't risk it alone."

"I don't feel alone like I used to. I'm taking your love with me to Annie.

I'm holding your love safely within me to give to our daughter. No matter what happens, our love will be enough."

He hung up the phone. The fading *clop-clop* of the horse pulling the Amish cart could be heard in the distance.

Robert's face was smeared with mud, and his hands were swollen and black. He knew he must have looked frightening in town as he ducked into his car. Riding up the first hill from Lowville and passing the Amish cart, he was rewarded with a nod and a shy smile from the wagon-riding family.

He drove along the Black River in view of the mountains, guarding their secrets, dangerous and seductive. He needed to cross the river in Boonville and take a familiar shortcut down Hawkinsville Road.

He drove as if an invisible time shredder was following him, chomping at his rear bumper and casting away all scenery in his rearview mirror. Passing the rock quarry, and then the A-frame cabins dotting the landscape between him and Snowbird Lake, meant that he could start counting the minutes. But he found himself closer than ever to the edge of an ancient forest, where time was measured by seasons and the water's flow.

The rain came in spurts. Then clouds thinned from what had looked like a mix of gray and black on a distorted X-ray. The sky narrowed in his vision as the forest walls climbed higher, encroaching on the road.

He turned onto the rutted logging road and ignored the trailer that had served as a focal point for the initial investigation. Steep hills slammed the rear bumper, scraping clumps of dirt. His front end bucked and splashed through potholes. He passed the last isolated cabin on the right, heading upstream parallel with the creek. He came to a flat iron bridge, brown water gushing underneath and lapping the edges. The water was still rising from the winter melt and recent rain.

He floored the pedal up the steep, winding hill underneath a canopy of pines. The car swayed back and forth until it made the crest. He took a deep breath and blinked away the sleep from his eyes.

Tree branches slapped the sides of his car like nature's gauntlet as the forest swallowed him whole. Silver droplets of water made the thick evergreens glow in a phosphorus light. His eyes darted for anything that matched the sketchbook in his seat.

He passed a stolen stop sign wedged in the crotch of a tree, and suddenly the road vanished. The stop sign appeared to be placed there as a warning, but more ominous was the fact that this unusual picture was perfectly sketched in Donna's notebook. He turned the pages until he found it. His heart hammered in his chest.

His vehicle landed over a deadfall tree, tires spinning hopelessly through dirt and air. Diving from the car, he jumped into the chaos of underbrush until he erupted into a clearing.

He saw a glimmer of water in the distance through leaves in the trees, and he followed a deer path along the ridge. His manic, hungry eyes searched through the forest for the house. He strained, stumbling, leaning forward. No sight of a house or cabin as he pushed through the jumble of undergrowth that soaked his pant legs.

He shivered as he walked, his teeth chattering along with the birds on the tree limbs above. His legs shuffled perilously close to the bluff above the water's edge, tripping and sometimes falling over old dead brush. The closer he got to the creek, the more he could see it meandering, navigating through a valley floor of bogs and swampy areas. As he kept shuffling, the path funneled wider until beneath tall limbs, he could see splashes of a painted green outline.

Tall cherry trees exploded with white and pinkish buds. The soiled green house stood in stark contrast to the rich excitement of nature's fresh colors.

From his angle, he could see a few windows with thick plastic nailed around the edges. The closer he got, the more he could see that the paint had worn thin streaks like old dry tears, as if the house had cried out. His nostrils widened and stiffened from the mildew and the pungent odor of old dead leaves. The only signs of life were field mice that darted under the crawl space.

As his eyes scanned the distance toward the creek, he noticed the wood scab of an opaque outhouse, worn like a sore in the wilderness. He almost walked into a generator hut, empty and rotted.

His feet slipped on wet, patchy ground. His back to the water, he faced a broken screen door. The door let out a loud whine. But nothing moved, not even a shadow on a wall. His eyes burned and blinked away at the diseased and emptied house.

With each step, what he saw and what he hoped to find collided in his fractured mind. He hoped to smell the scent of her favorite cherry perfume, or to see the flash of her scared body running and ducking for a corner to hide. All he saw was an abandoned home, left for crawling forms of life.

The place reeked of wet odors, from dead rodents to the rotting wood inside the parchment walls. There was an old stove littered with mouse droppings, and bottles and caps were strewn across the counter of a double sink.

Robert walked on broken glass, and the cold knifed through him in this dank place as if it were grown inside and farmed out to an evil world. His body shook from his core in seismic tremors. His tongue felt parched, dipped in chalk. His mouth twitched and his voice shuddered as he formed helpless words to speak.

His own words startled him, and every time he formed "Ann—," as he finished his plea, it sounded like a bird innocently chirping her name. He shifted from one abandoned room to the next. A pinhole of hope closed with each vacant room. No echo. Only his hollow, strained call dissipating into a sinkhole of dead ends.

One last door beckoned him, one with a diamond-shaped glass handle. He pulled on the loose handle, and his gaze sharpened. A twin bed with a soiled mattress. His heart jumped in his chest. Handcuffs dangled around the head post. The only window was boarded with wood. A dresser of peeling blue paint was the only furniture on a plain subfloor.

He walked over to a closet in an even darker corner of the room, holding his trembling hand in front of his face, afraid of what he might find.

He felt a nylon bag, bulging at the seams. An old-looking white robe, thin as a hospital gown, hung down from a hook in the closet. The corner was so dark that he held one last sliver of hope that Annie might surface from a blind spot deep in the closet.

His reddened eyes blinked several times to be sure of what he saw. He dragged the backpack out into the natural light from the open door. "Yes. Oh God, yes." It was Annie's backpack.

He dragged it over to the bed where there was a ring of dried blood, a crimson outline. He choked back tears and dried his face.

When he opened the pack, most of her notebooks spilled out, unchanged from the day she disappeared. He fumbled further and felt her small New Testament wedged at the bottom of the pack. He held up the black leather Bible and began flipping through pages. His heart shot into his throat when a family photo fell out onto the floor. It skidded along in the cold draft, stopping just past his muddy shoes. He picked it up, pinching it between his thumb and forefinger, and noticed the date on the back. August 13, 1988.

He looked back down on the bed and noticed something about the black-and-white spotted composition notebook. In bold blue capital letters was written *DIARY*.

In the first few pages, the days leading up to her disappearance were written down. All the excitement she had felt in preparing to start middle school with her friends. How she had just gotten new school clothes and her new backpack. His red eyes stung as he blinked through the tears to read it. There were blank pages and gaps, then the diary started again.

The writing was sometimes faint and scratchy, a cry for help to her family and to God. As he read about her captivity and the meager surroundings, his eyes watered the book with wet hot tears. He fought through the stinging blindness. He had to finish it, and he had to know where it would take him.

She wrote about her incredible fear, shackled to her bed, in the pitch-black darkness, listening to mice scurrying across the floor. Some details were too horrific for his mind to swallow, like the shadow of the creeper coming over her. He flushed some evil details from his mind to survive reading to the end.

He kept on until his fingers tightly gripped the very last page. *My stomach was on fire. They said I have an infection…I begged for help…I'm sweating…I blacked out. Mommy, where are you? Daddy, hold me . . .*

He turned away and fell to the floor with a thud, moaning like a cat caught in a claw trap. Wiping the spittle from his mouth, he pulled his legs into his chest and then pulled himself back on the bed.

The last and final words came as if she had found a final reservoir of strength igniting her mind, a last flash of brilliant saving grace. They were the words of her fleeting soul singing like the morning birds seeking the sun.

I will always be in the sunshine and in the pearly drops of rain. So where you are I am never lost. Hear the baby in me cry, Mommy and Daddy? They say no tears in heaven, only joy. They say no faith in heaven, only love. I will be waiting for you in heaven with my joy, with all my LOVE. I know the light is coming for me.

He fell back on the mattress and the ceiling spun. His body and his mind caved in, shrunk down, as if withered, ripened beyond use. He cradled the diary and tucked his knees toward his chin.

In his dream, she called to him from the other shore. This time, by some miracle, whether introduced by God into his ragged mind or not, he swiftly cut across the thin frozen lake and held her tightly. He gave her a hug like the one they shared together on the concrete steps of the church, but this time as he twirled with her, suddenly she was gone.

He looked up at the endless sky to see that she was being tugged, pulled into heavenly currents, to a celestial shore.

The sheriff and his young partner pursued the pastor's trail. They dug in near the tree with the stop sign; they saw his car stuck over a log. Tom felt the hood of the car with the palm of his hand: slightly warm. Guns drawn, they rushed down the path until they found the green house.

Robert Davis heard a muffled sound in his dream, until the distant shouts pulled him back to the bed. They burst through the doorway and found him, curled around the diary.

What they didn't know was that he had found the last best part of Annie. He had found the exit of her soul, the place where her spirit took flight, the part of her that could not be broken, and the part of her that nourished his starving heart.

Twenty-Three
Where the Best Flowers Grow

Splitting gravel beneath the wheels of his police car, Tom Brower drove around the circle drive to the door of the Davis home. Face drained of color, his eyes wandering to the distance across a field of dandelions, he returned to his reflection in the mirror. Tugging the rim of his hat, he hardly recognized himself anymore. The missing-person case of Annie Davis, the long winter, and recent events had deepened the ashen lines of his face. With one last grip on the wheel, he let go a deep sigh, blowing air through his mustache.

It was time. He released the wheel and clutched the notebook full of pictures.

Annie had been found in the ice-cold depths of Snowbird Lake, amazingly intact. They found her in the black silt, her body frozen through the winter, preserved to a degree. A reasonable guess from the initial autopsy was that she had lived about a year after her abduction and then was killed, deposited in the lake. It was a preliminary autopsy report, and not all the test results had come back from the lab.

Hardly a happy respite for the family, but the image of her face, hair, and eyes helped them to remember the way she was. Brower had watched the sturdy approach of the Davis family toward the casket in the graveyard. But he had wanted to wait for them to absorb the impact that she had been found in the lake, have a degree of closure, before he showed them these revealing pictures about Ray Underwood. He knew it would only deepen the lines on their faces like those of an oak tree on a windy ridge.

It was supposed to rain the day of the funeral, but it hadn't. The temperatures warmed enough for short sleeves, and the leaves on the trees thickened to an emerald green. Flowers sprouted along the grooved lines of the path to the coffin. Eleven-year-old Rob knelt down and picked some wild-flowers and brought them to his sister's casket. When the final prayer had been said, he gently released the clumps of flowers from his hand into the coal-black dirt. Someone said that day, "Annie was the most beautiful flower of all, and now she lives where the roses never fade."

The sheriff pulled his mind back to his duty. He had to tell them the startling news, and he couldn't wait any longer for fear they would hear it on a local station. It had only been a few days since the funeral, but he had no choice. He knew their son would be in school by now, and he could sit with Mary and Pastor Davis in the kitchen.

He unlatched the door, secured the notebook under his arm, and leaned into the sun. Closing his eyes for a moment, he stood and allowed the sun to massage his face. He was ready to release the burden he carried.

Ringing the doorbell, he politely stepped back off the stoop, hearing feet pacing for the door. As the door opened, a cool breeze came between him and the pastor.

"Tom." Robert offered him a surprised but weary look. He indicated his jogging apparel. "Doctor told me I needed to start walking."

"Pastor, are you on some heart regimen?""

"The doctor suggested an aspirin a day too. He called it a miracle drug. Maybe I'm the only one he says that to."

"Sorry, but…I…um…I needed to talk to you both, so you're not blind-sided by any news that might leak out."

Robert's face tightened, and he dropped his head. The sheriff heard Mary shuffling in the background. "What is it?" she asked in a sleepy voice.

"Tom is here, honey!" The pastor's neck stiffened.

"There are certain things you both need to know. You need to hear it from me first."

Mary drew beside her husband, hands on her hips, wearing a long vanilla cotton dress. The curvature of the baby was taking shape underneath, as if she was wearing a curtain waiting for the opening act. "Tom, absolutely, you come into the kitchen and help us drink some coffee."

Her generous spirit, even after all she'd been through, struck a profound familial chord within him, and Brower felt tears fill his eyes as he slipped off his hat and fingered his tangled hair.

Robert put his arm around Mary for a moment, attempting to compose himself. The three of them stood exactly where they had in December of last year, prepared to step forward a few paces to the kitchen where a serious conversation about Annie's disappearance had rallied them.

Robert pulled one of the red vinyl chairs out for Tom.

Mary slipped over to pour coffee. Her hair was slicked back into a pony-tail, and strands of gray were contrasted against the small, sunlit window.

Robert pulled back a chair for her as he sat down, prepared to face the sheriff. Mary poured the hot steamy coffee into a special mug for Tom before she took her seat.

"Mary, you're a saint," he said, offering a firm smile. "Aren't you supposed to be on bed rest?"

"Any more horizontal for me, and I might be in a coma."

"When is the baby due?"

She blushed, revealing a lovely blossoming, not entirely the same woman who had sunk into a black well of despair. "The baby is due early September. A good time for harvest, wouldn't you say, Tom?"

Tom Brower nodded shyly and took a sip of coffee, working it under his mustache. His elbows leaned on the table, the notebook in front of him.

The pastor folded his arms and sighed, eyes wandering, foot nervously tapping the floor.

Mary bravely looked toward him, arching her back to get comfortable.

"My wife is making a baby blanket for you," Tom said.

"How nice! I can't wait to see it." Mary's eyes shone.

"I got some pictures I need to show you," he said, and took another sip of coffee.

The pastor shook his head. Mary lifted her hands to her face. "No, Tom. Not pictures of Annie."

"Sorry. No. Not pictures of Annie."

Robert leaned in, unfolding his arms and reaching out to clasp his wife's hand.

Tom opened the notebook full of pictures and notes. "The night Donna took her life, we searched the apartment. It didn't take long to find some telling pictures." He didn't say anything else; he plucked out the first picture, an instant Polaroid flash. It was Donna in one of those old picture booths. She was sitting on Ray Underwood's lap.

Robert instantly recognized the two and sprang from his chair, clutching his chest.

Mary put her hands to her trembling lips. "Oh no, they…they were lovers?"

Tom spread more pictures on the table—Ray and Donna together: hiking through the woods, holding hands on Mount McCauley in front of a sign overlooking the mountain range. Then there was a picture of them at a classic car show in Boonville.

"She told me she had a boyfriend when I asked her why she moved to Dutch Hollow. I questioned why she came here in the first place, because it was odd moving here as if she were your self-appointed psychic. But then, that meeting in the gazebo, I just felt sorry for her. A pathetic creature, pretending she had a boyfriend but sitting there by herself. I did some research and found she had lived alone with her mother until her early thirties."

The pastor put his arm around his wife. "How long were they an item?"

Mary looked up to him from her chair, and then to Tom. "Was she stalking us?"

Tom leaned in. "Their relationship goes beyond the last few years. I did some more research and found out Ray Underwood went to prison for about six months when he was nineteen. His own father saw to it. He served time for the horrible abuse he dished out to his siblings, torturing his younger brothers and likely raping his own sister."

Pastor Davis stood up, folding his arms, staring out the window.

"Prison letters. I have some of those too." He spread them on the kitchen table.

Mary sobbed through her hands. Her husband sat down and tried to console her.

"I'm sorry, but the news people have been chomping on my rear all week."

The pastor leaned in. "You had no choice, Tom. I wouldn't have…we wouldn't have wanted it any other way. We want to know everything, and we want to hear it from you."

"We don't know that she was directly involved in Annie's disappearance.

What we think is that she got taken in by him in a jailhouse romance and then in some ways got entangled with perhaps a few other unsolved cases too. We may never know the full extent of her involvement."

Pastor Davis hugged his wife. She cried into his shoulder. "So it made her the perfect psychic," he said.

"Could be. She seemed to have a history of uncanny abilities, but who's to say a psychic or medium wouldn't cross the wrong side of the law, maybe lonely enough, manipulated, or both."

Tom gathered up his pictures. "You folks have seen enough. I don't think there will be any more surprises now."

Mary hugged Tom. And Robert did something he'd never done with the sheriff. He, too, gave him a hug, and thanked him again.

They cried together, but it felt like the freedom of a dam breaking, consuming a scarred emotional landscape, a sweet release, allowing the current to have its way.

Annie was a rose hidden beneath the winter snow, but now she had the spring, a place for them to rally and remember her.

Twenty-Four

The Delivery

n the delivery room, Mary screamed in pain. Robert dutifully paced off the room with a worried look. The baby wasn't due for weeks, but she was determined to push headlong, bravely into her new world.

Contractions had been coming so fast before they got there that he ran several red lights, afraid the baby would be born on the floorboard of the car.

Several staff members had joined them in the lobby, and Mary seemed to be in numerous capable hands. One blue-clad staff member had placed her in a wheelchair, and then a team crowded the elevator to the third floor. They rushed her into the delivery room and helped Mary undress, propped her on the bed with legs up, ready and waiting for the doctor who phoned that he was on his way but stuck in traffic. It seemed this team had everything under control, except for who should stay behind in the room and continue to monitor her contractions. The room had emptied as if they were having a meeting about who should stay and who should go on break.

Mary's water broke, and suddenly Robert was looking down at his wife, feeling stuck between the call button and the doorway. He looked under the sheet and saw what he feared. This child was crowning. He felt like a ninth-inning catcher pulled from an empty dugout without enough time to swallow his fear. As he looked sidelong a second time, he yelled from a crouch, "Somebody! Help! She's having the baby!" Ready hands sweating profusely, he screamed louder than an umpire. "Somebody! Nurse! Anybody out there?"

He finally got the staff's attention, and the cavalry came from both sides of the door. The nurses watched a baby plunging from the womb. One nurse yelled, "Get the doctor, fast!"

Robert looked up, his arms cradled and waiting to receive the child, his face drained of blood. To his relief, the nurses removed him from his backup position.

And then he had a moment, an ugly epiphany, when he thought, *God, how can I protect this one? She almost fell to the floor on her first trip into this world.*

As the baby cried and joy erupted, the father felt a brief stab at losing Annie. He hoped this new birth would mark a healing transition, stitching together the wounds beneath the skin one loving thread at a time.

Amanda Kaye Davis was born ready, a spitfire bundle of five pounds and two ounces. Perhaps some wondered how much she would resemble Annie, but her parents knew she wasn't coming into the world to take Annie's place. She did favor her mother in many ways: strawberry-blonde hair, button nose, and a slender frame. She was God's offering of grace. Mary's exhausted, perspiring face glowed as a nurse placed the bundle of wonder in her arms.

It was a new beginning for his family, and Robert couldn't wait to find Rob down the hall and break the news. For the first time since he could remember, he hugged his son with a depth of passion that he hadn't known existed anymore.

Leaving, they held hands. They had unfinished business. He recruited Rob to help him fix Annie's room and turn it into a baby nursery. Rob didn't mind. He enjoyed spending more time with his father—a real dad and not the sorry man drowning in his own sorrow. They should have changed the room over sooner, but now he would make up for lost time—on Annie's room and with his son. Rob liked the new normal.

Robert and his son went home, and after dinner they sat together on Annie's old bed, creating a plan. Empty boxes lay beside the bed where they had been for weeks now. There was no turning back. A healthy baby and an eager mother couldn't wait to get home. What had been a shrine, left alone for two years, was changed on that day. The Cabbage Patch dolls, the rainbow posters on the wall, the trinkets on her dresser, and the various Girl Scout awards were all tenderly placed in boxes. Family photos with Annie were left on the dresser; someday Amanda would learn the loving story of her big sister.

The bed was shoved to one side, making room for a crib and a changing station. Finally, Rob and his dad secured a windup toy displaying the full range of the universe: from the sun to the planets, stars, moon, and then in the midst of it all, an angel watching over the earth. Winding it up, they both happily lost themselves in the planetary motions.

Amanda. The name meant "worthy of love," and it was a newfound message igniting Robert's heart to share with the world, an eternal torch chasing the darkness.

As time would have it, her love shone so brightly he was sometimes blinded by it. He could hardly expect to see the unexpected miracle that would soon cross his path.

Twenty-Five
Tried by Fire

Golden waves of corn stretched and yawned on lofty hills. A variety of garden vegetables were displayed on sun-splashed stands along the pastor's route from his hometown to Rome, New York. It was harvesttime.

Crimson leaves shifted and scattered beneath the humming of his tires. It was a warm and windy fall day. Maple trees blushed violet-red and pumpkin-orange, dressing up the blue horizon.

The loss of Annie didn't slap at his heart as much anymore. Baby Amanda's dimpled smile, wondrous blue eyes, and lust for life kept his blood flowing. His heart was on the mend.

He thought of how easy it would have been to escape to the hills and further, to the mountains he now saw in his rearview mirror. He could have retired. He could have hidden behind the wreckage of his own life. But he hadn't taken that journey. Somehow, he had found his clerical footing and forward momentum.

He liked the city of Rome. It had character and historical charm. The Erie Canal had smooth, worn paths, and one could imagine donkeys pulling the boats from yesteryear along the deep water. Further in town, more signs of a faded era were evident. Even the shattered, broken windows of redbrick buildings along the canal told the story of a former industrial revolution where textiles were manufactured and shipped around the world. In the center of town, Fort Stanwick reminded everyone of a day further back in time, when the colonists repelled the British in the Revolutionary War. A huge picture of Paul Revere riding his horse had been painted across the wide girth of a building in brilliant red, white, and blue.

Pastor Davis had his calling to do. He needed to visit a former member of the church at a nursing home. He felt the anguish of this lonely man, having lost ties with family members, plodding out the remainder of his existence as if herded along, shuffled beyond a gate, waiting for a sterilized death.

Driving over the tracks and feeling the rumble beneath him caused Robert to focus on his immediate surroundings. He blinked and slowed to a crawl, pulling over to the side of the road where a slapdash bunch of trailer homes existed on a property that looked more like a junkyard. Many times he had passed this way, not bothering to think about the aimless, dirt-faced kids who lived here and walked a path of boredom. But today gave him pause, a place in his heart that wasn't there before.

He took a deep breath, rubbing his eyes. He thought he saw smoke billowing, as if this one ramshackle trailer had a vent. Eyes wide, he saw the lick of a flame through a kitchen window. The sun sparkled through limp trees from the edge of the park, creating untamed reflections on the tin roofing. But this was different. He stopped, wheels crunching into the gravel.

His heart sped. His eyes stretched. Yes, it was a fire.

From yards away he saw the curling, consuming fire flame up in a window as if mocking him, teasing his resolve. There was no hesitation in his driving onto the lot. If anyone was inside, there wasn't much time to act.

As the pastor rolled down the window, he could hear the fire's consuming whine. He leaped from his car. Eyes wide, he saw the fire swallowing parts of a kitchen, melting a counter. Sparks flew, snaps and pops shot like firecrackers. Smoke billowed from every crevice.

A young man from a nearby trailer noticed the towering smoke too. He stumbled from his door, wiping the sleep from his eyes. He scampered toward the pastor, a cigarette dangling from his lips but a portable phone in his hand. He was shirtless, his chest sunken, wearing cut-off jeans and seemingly mesmerized by the fire as the cigarette dribbled from his lips.

Robert turned to him and said, "Call 911! Now! Better put that cigarette out too."

As the man dialed 911, the cigarette tumbled from his mouth and he extinguished it with the toe of his sandal.

Robert raced toward the door, alone. He heard the voices of other people gathering outside as he felt the heat of the door. A woman yelled, "There are children in that house!"

He turned the doorknob with the sleeve of his jacket. Smoke billowed out, racing into his lungs and making him cough. He fell to his knees, at the mercy of the fire, which flamed higher and danced with new zeal from the oxygen-fed open doorway.

His eyes stung as if there were red-hot pokers stabbing at him; he shaded them from the heat. From his knees he searched the flame as it consumed the linoleum in a wave of fire. But within its frothing appetite, the fire brought a light. He saw them: the girl looked about ten years old, holding her infant brother in diapers in the hall across from the fire.

The girl's face was covered in ashes, black-ringed eyes blinking toward him in horror. She barely held the baby, struggling to stay on her feet. She stumbled toward him.

Lungs burning, voice squeezed of air, he cried in short bursts, "Come now! Run to me! Run to me!" She ran and tripped over the breezeway, collapsing into his arms.

He scooped them both up and ran outside, falling into the fresh air on a patch of grass. Hacking a few times, gasping for air, he looked at the baby. The boy was blackened by the smoke and not breathing. He blew into the baby's lungs. The child coughed and cried back to life.

The girl leaned on her knees, pounding her fist, trying to talk, mouthing words. Her pink swollen lips dripped with phlegm and spit. She slammed her knees violently, attempting to talk, but her words hung like dead skin inside her mouth.

Robert heard fire trucks in the distance and watched the flames envelop the right side of the house, drawing closer to the propane tanks only a few yards away. He gathered everyone up. Others from the park circled them. Someone took the baby from his arms and cleared the infant's mouth of soot with a dishrag.

As they fell into the crowd the young girl took her blackened hand and yanked the pastor's sleeve. "My…my sis…ter still…" Bent over, she gasped for air. "She's in…inside!"

The horror of it beat like a jackhammer in his heart. "Are you sure?"

A round plum of a woman ambled forward in a blue bathrobe. "She's right! She's right!"

Robert heard the howling sirens on the road. He looked into the girl's frightened eyes and clasped her shoulders. "What's her name? What's her name?" He just needed a name.

"Miranda!" she belted out.

"Tell him how old she is, Melissa," the woman pleaded, hugging her.

"She's five!"

He started for the door, but this time the flames were there to greet him.

"Wait! Wait!" He heard shouts. The young man in cut-off jeans had taken the lady's bathrobe and doused it with water.

"Here," he shouted, and threw it on the pastor.

The woman stood in her nightgown, revealing folds of flesh. Wearing her bathrobe over his head like some manic monk, Robert looked back and saw tears spilling from the woman's face as she made the sign of the cross.

"You were meant for this!" she said. "Save her!" Others watched with gaping mouths of horror.

He lunged through the breach of the fiery doorway. The fire didn't shrink from his clerical title. When he dropped in, he found that hell had no social barriers. It didn't care that he was a man of the cloth. His fabric was good tinder.

As the flames jumped higher, he fell to the floor, choking and crawling while the sirens blared closer.

The smoke stung, blinding him, keeping his face to the floor. Charcoal smoke surrounded him. He snaked on his belly, attempting to find air pockets. He snorted, shouting from his contorted mouth. "Miranda! Miranda!"

No answer. The only place he had left to search was the master bedroom. No hope of life anywhere else.

Tears stung red, his face sucking dirty air from the floor. *Please God! Please let me find her!*

"Miranda! Come to my voice!"

He felt the doorway. "Miranda! Trust me. I'll save you. Please! Let me save you. God, let me save her!" He snorted tears and mucus.

His lungs burned, choking him from the inside. But in a moment, in a flash between the snap and snarl of the fire, he heard a whimper, a faint cry. He crawled toward the sniffling sounds. When he found a broom closet, the sound rang joy to his burning ears.

He pulled her to his chest—a black thumb in her mouth, black soot on her face. She dragged a naked baby doll missing a leg. He wrapped them in the bathrobe.

The fire collapsed around them, and the doorway of the room melted. He was passing out, blinking into the black face of death.

His scorching eyes searched for an exit. As he held Miranda in the thick grip of his hands, he saw the smoke-fogged outline of the bedroom window. He knew what he had to do—break the window or die trying.

Shards of glass exploded on impact. They tumbled outside.

As he rolled on the ground with Miranda wound in the blue bathrobe, smoke rose from the flesh of his arms. He looked up in a daze. The crowd looked on as if they were junkies, transfixed, getting an adrenaline rush from the chaos of fire.

Robert felt the thick forearms of firemen pulling at him, dragging him away from the fire. Then—a blast.

The house exploded, raining fire and debris. His eyes fell away into darkness.

Twenty-Six
A Promised Seed

Mary was cleaning Annie's black marble headstone with vinegar and a sponge. Baby Amanda slept, sunbathing on a blanket on the soft, worn grass. As Mary swiped the sponge across the carved letters of her daughter's name, she thought, *It would have been a nice day for an early fall picnic, girls only.*

Her deepest thoughts were suddenly broken by the rumbling of wheels churning over gravel along the grooved path of the cemetery. It was Tom Brower. No flashing lights or sirens, but she knew it had to be important for him to create a cloud of dust.

Mary dropped the sponge and sprang to her feet, brushing the dirt from her slacks. She watched with quickened breath as the four-wheel-drive vehicle came to a halt a few yards away.

Tom Brower jumped out, twisting an ankle on a clump of grass. He limped forward with his hat in hand, trying to look respectful despite his entrance. A moderate breeze caught and lifted his mousy brown hair as he squared his shoulders in front of her.

Her lips quivered, but she spoke first. "What is it, Tom?"

"Mary. It's about Robert."

She fell to her knees, reaching for Amanda as if his long shadow suddenly spelled another disaster. She gathered up the baby in her arms, but kept to her knees. She looked up at him with a twisted mouth. No words. She had no words.

"He's in the hospital, in serious but stable condition."

"But…he's going to be okay?" She gulped, attempting not to cry.

"He saw this fire in a trailer park just outside Rome. You know how he is. He couldn't wait, and a good thing too…"

"What do you mean?" Her eyes searched beyond the ancient and slanted graves, far above the ridge into a wide blue sky.

"Mary, he saved three children today." Tears welled up in his eyes.

Mary doubled over, groaning. Amanda reached up and grabbed her nose. The baby watched and then fingered the tears running down her mother's cheeks.

"Thank God he's okay."

"I should take you, Mary."

"I want my son." She stood up with Amanda in the carrier and brushed off her pant legs.

"We can drive to school first," he said. "I'll escort you all the way. It's the least I can do."

"Okay," she said, voice trailing away.

Tom Brower drove the Davis family to the Rome city hospital, passing by the same buildings Pastor Davis had driven by earlier that day. He made the trip in a matter of minutes.

They pulled into the circle drive near the emergency doors and piled out. Rob was composed and helpful, having played with the baby and given his mother a chance to pray. She looked down and smiled at him, rubbing his brown, shiny hair. She noted how his features grew more like his father's every day.

When they all came off the second-floor elevator, they noticed a dark-haired little girl with a bandage on her forehead being wheeled down the corridor by a young woman who looked to be in her thirties. Tom Brower excused himself and sat down on a bench in the hall. "This is your time," he said politely.

As she approached her husband's door, Mary watched in surprise as the young woman turned into her husband's room. The wheelchair-bound daughter smiled, eyes darting about as she gripped her balloons.

Mary held Amanda wrapped in a blanket and steadily headed for the doorway. Rob followed beside her. They dipped their heads into the door, but at first her husband didn't appear to notice them.

Robert was propped up in bed near a large sunlit window. Mary could tell he was delighted to have unexpected new guests.

As the nurse was leaving, she smiled at Mary and put her finger out for little Amanda to grab. "You have an adorable baby girl." As she walked away, she said, "That's the little girl who was rescued today, and her mom."

Mary held Rob back, watching the scene unfold. Tears streamed down her face.

The young mother collapsed on Robert, sobbing. The astonished pastor looked up to see his wife and son. Overwhelmed with emotion, his eyes brimmed with tears as the young woman cried inconsolably over his bed.

The little girl in the wheelchair seemed cheerful enough, but as she wrestled with her balloons, suddenly she lost one. Pastor Davis raised his bandaged arms in a futile attempt to rescue it. The red balloon drifted calmly over his head to the ceiling, where it seemed prepared to spend the day.

The mother squared up and spoke to her youngest daughter. "Miranda, this is the man who saved your life. No matter what, no matter how old you get, I don't want you to ever forget him. Promise me, honey, not to ever forget this man."

The little girl firmly nodded her head up and down.

Mary tried to choke back her own tears and drew closer with her children, watching the wonderful wide gleam grow in the little girl's eyes. "Thanks for saving Emily," the girl said as she held up the charred one-legged doll.

"You are most welcome, honey. You were a brave little girl to trust me like that."

The mother seemed satisfied that she'd made her point. "I need to get back to my other children," she said. "They are recovering and being cared for on another floor."

Mary sensed the young woman had some explaining to do about how her children had been left home alone. But to Mary, the single mother seemed profoundly changed and ready to defend her God-given rights.

As Mary watched the mother and child leave, she felt a wellspring of admiration for her husband. She was glad to have captured this moment and wanted to cherish it for the rest of her life.

Mary walked over and placed baby Amanda on her father's chest. "Does it hurt?"

"Oh, it stings a little." He wrapped his bandaged arms around his daughter. "They tried to wrap me up like a mummy, but I told them you wouldn't recognize me if they did." He stroked Rob's shiny hair.

Rob leaned on him. "It looks like you were in a wicked fight."

"Yes," he said. "You should have seen what the other guy looked like."

Mary leaned over, showering him with hugs and kisses. "Promise me a safe and boring life from now on."

"I've never felt better, hon, but they do have to keep me for observation. And they're checking my heart."

Mary blinked away the tears.

The sheriff ambled into the room, limping on his tender ankle. "You know, friend, there's a fine line between foolishness and bravery. But this time you have forever blurred that line."

The pastor sat up to shake Tom's hand with his good one. "Hey, Tom. I feel pretty good, but I have to tell you, I think when all the medicine wears off, I'm gonna hurt in places I didn't know I had."

"You keep leading with that big heart like you do, and that's all that'll be left of you," said Tom. "I bet in a few days, you'll have those raggedy old sneakers on again."

"Was that a compliment, Tom?"

"Lately, I've been just trying to keep you out of the news." Tom turned toward the window and let the air whistle through his mustache. He seemed to be searching for something, something beyond the opaque buildings, beyond the auburn trees, beyond the deep blue sky.

Mary took a long breath. She thought that perhaps Tom felt guilty, as if he had let them down somehow. She had a mind to tell him it was time to give it to God and just let it go. "It's okay, Tom. You did all you could do for Annie."

Twenty-Seven
Catch and Release

Trout fishing in the fall can be a formidable challenge. The fish are wary of human footsteps and not so easily enticed with fancy-tied flies.

Tom Brower drove past the small but robust town of Remsen toward his favorite fishing hole. The creek ran from the main road through thick undergrowth until the woodland divided into rolling hills and green pastures. An asphalt farm road knifed through the countryside, leading him to a single-lane bridge where he often found a pleasant escape from a demanding job.

Holding his fly rod above his head, he slipped into the chilly spine of the creek. The cold swell of the water tugged at his olive-colored hip boots. Autumn leaves flirted in the breeze from a creek-bed tree. A solitary crimson leaf floated past him, dancing on the rippling current. Nature came alive, and he enjoyed its company.

Tom raised his fly rod to the one o'clock position, snapping his line in a whipping *s* motion in the crisp autumn air. He let the slack grow and hum between his thumb and forefinger until it reached the honey hole. The tied fly broke the surface of a swell over a dead tree fall. He looked for the flash of a tail, a silver speck, a gleam of life in the water, hoping to set the hook at just the right moment.

He wasn't there for the delicate meat of the native brook trout. It was the splash of life, the matching of wits, the desire to subdue nature that made his heart thump hard.

He snapped the line. The rod bent and the fish twisted in the water. He patiently allowed the trout to wear himself down. Carefully removing the hook from the lip of the fish, he cradled the trout in his hands and then gently released it into the stream. He offered the bronze trophy a new lease on life.

It was a good day to let his mind drift with the current and let the water soothe his tired mind. It had been a few weeks since he'd seen the Davis family in the hospital. He had kept all of Annie's pictures, including the sketchbook that Pastor Davis confessed to taking from Donna's apartment and a copy of the completed and unabridged autopsy report written on long legal pages. He even had the diary Annie had kept during her captivity in the forest. It was all in a nondescript box in the back of his vehicle.

With everyone dead, the case was closed. He shouldn't have kept that carton in the back, with all its pieces of a sad, tragic puzzle. It belonged somewhere locked away, sealed forever. Some secrets were better left in hell.

A stiff cold wind picked up in the creek, and his exploration of eddies and breaks in the water would have to wait until next year. He turned headlong into the first breath of winter. The seasonal transfer of nature's power was in full swing.

He climbed toward his vehicle and eyed the forest line where the limbs bowed and released their tender leaves to God's threshing floor.

Slipping from his waders and placing his shoes on, he reached into the backseat one more time. On top of the box was the tattered picture of Annie. Her bright brown eyes, full of wonder, looked directly into him with a piercing hope that wouldn't let him forget, filling his mind with what-ifs. What if he had paid more attention to Donna in the first place? Could he have saved Annie? According to the autopsy, she likely wasn't alive when Donna had first made herself known. He whistled beneath his mustache, lost in a world where men are only made of clay, where they one day fall away, crumbling into dust. He wiped a solitary tear from his face and opened the glove box, placing the picture inside where he would keep her sacred memory.

He thumbed through the items and came across the diary. Tears filled his eyes as he read the final pages. *Drowning in my tears. Help. This child in me cries for you. God help me.*

It struck a familiar chord. Tom Brower thought about his two girls, teenagers in high school. What if it happened to one of them? He set the diary in the front seat. It belonged to the Davis family. They had the right to do what they pleased with it. They could burn it or they could bury it next to Annie.

Snug in his truck in the middle of the afternoon, he served himself some lukewarm coffee from his thermos. Looking around at the beautifully carved roads that threaded through hilly woods, it occurred to him that Donna had grown up nearby. Just then, a random thought hooked his mind. His heart raced back in time, thinking about the words in Annie's diary. He had promised the Davis family that he would tell them everything, but he just couldn't tell them about the acid that had been poured into her lower extremities or the final details of the autopsy report. It was as if somehow Ray Underwood had thought he could cleanse or hide his deepest perversion. Yet, the thought of not telling the Davis family everything in the report felt like a slow acidic leak burning a growing hole in his haunted memory of events.

Then he realized. He had the address written down from when he had photocopied the old news report about the teenage psychic. Donna was in a black-and-white photo, standing on the front porch. In the photo you could see the hard, narrow eyes of her mother, folding her arms in the background while the reporters talked to her daughter about the solved case of a missing neighbor boy.

He knew it was in the box. He groped around until he lifted the picture from the bottom of the pile. He turned it over, and sure enough, on the blank side he had scribbled the address: 401 Plank Road, Remsen, New York.

The road was only minutes away, and he easily found the turn along the deep wood line of tall oaks and thickly knotted maple trees. The light from the sky narrowed under the auburn colors. He spied sparsely dotted homes set back deep in the woods where folks treasured their privacy. He watched the left side, waiting for the number to appear. As he drove down a knoll, an old ranch house appeared on a ridge, but not too far from the road. His number matched the black mailbox at the bottom of the drive.

Tom parked along the edge of the road as leaves skittered from the wake of his car. He pulled Annie's picture from the glove box. Clutching it in his hand, he walked up the gravel drive.

The house sat in the shade of the woods. It seemed empty of life as he drew closer, near an old, sunken porch. The same porch, the same old white, round columns. They all bore the same markings as the picture, only now the house was weathered and chipped of paint.

Tom knocked on the door, but no answer. He knocked a few more times, but only a rustling of the leaves could be heard, and then a cold silence. As he trudged down the driveway, he told himself, *Time to let go.*

He hopped in the Land Rover and fired up the engine, shaking his head. Perhaps he'd been chasing his own demons over real clues. After all, the lead investigator on the case had interviewed Donna's mother once they found out that Donna knew Underwood.

But Annie's diary…certain phrases caught at him, whispering something he couldn't quite hear.

Was Annie trying to tell her parents something without her captors noticing it? Could there have been someone else involved, besides Ray Underwood and Donna Brushton? Could Donna's mother possibly have had anything to do with Annie in that green scab of a house in the woods? He felt foolish for imagining that the woman harbored any secrets. It had been a far-fetched idea that had hooked his mind, and now he tried to shake it loose. As he drove away and the car caught another rise, he glanced back in his rearview mirror.

Slamming his brakes, screeching to a halt, he caught a glimpse of someone. The flash of a zipper, perhaps from a small jacket.

Tom backed up twenty yards, flashers blinking. Walking softly from his vehicle, he stepped through shifting leaves beneath the shade of thick branches, holding Annie's picture in his hand.

His eyes narrowed on a raggedy little girl wearing an oversized pink jacket. She looked to be slightly more than a year old. She stumbled between piles of leaves and didn't notice him drawing closer to her.

Then a broad-shouldered woman with salt-and-pepper hair appeared from behind a tree with a rake in her hand. "Who are you?" she snorted.

He ignored her for a moment, transfixed on the girl, having forgotten he was out of uniform.

The little girl plopped down in a pile of leaves close to the back door of the house. She had a small nose, sparkling round brown eyes, and locks of hair like a Shirley Temple doll.

Hand trembling in the chilly wind, he held the picture at arm's length, targeting his gaze on the little girl. She looked exactly as he would imagine Annie might look at that age. The little girl lifted her eyes toward him as she wiped her runny nose on the sleeve of her jacket.

The woman stood between him and the girl as if ready to defend her territory with a rake. "I'm calling the police."

Tom flashed his badge. "Oneida Sheriff's Department, ma'am."

"Just what do you want?" She looked at him with sober, anxious eyes.

"This your daughter?"

"Absolutely not. I'm her grandmother."

"How old is she?"

"What's this all about? She's more than a year old."

"Where is your daughter?" He baited her with his words, a line of questions carefully stringing themselves out to entice her.

She swallowed an invisible knot. "Donna passed away, and I've been raising her child."

"Sorry, ma'am, but I have to ask. How'd she die?"

"Childbirth."

She'd taken his words and run the line. Now he needed to pull it tight, set the hook, and watch her squirm.

"I'd say that part about childbirth might just be true, but it wasn't Donna, was it?"

The blood drained from her face.

"In fact, Donna took her own life," he said.

She stood, mouth wide open.

"We have a new thing called DNA. It's remarkable how we all have our own set of codes that tell us exactly who we belong to."

With trembling hands, the woman reached to take the small child from the pile of leaves. "Come on, Charity."

He grabbed her arm before she could reach the child. Charity looked bewildered, as if lost in the wilderness and about to cry. He crouched down next to the little girl. "You look just like your mother." And then, he felt the sad warmth of her innocence flood his very soul.

At long last he had what remained of Annie; a part of her that still lived on, a part of her that had cried out when all hope was gone.

Epilogue

Ninth-grade English class, and Mrs. Brooks is writing descriptive phrases on the blackboard, telling us how some words make the mind's eye come alive. I watch as she punishes a clean piece of chalk with her determined fingers.

"Amanda." She turns to me with deep lines forming on her brow, her eyes targeting me from above her wide-rimmed glasses.

Since she knows I want to be a writer, she expects a healthy response. I hide my nerves beneath a grin and constrict the pencil in my hand. "Yes, simple really. A simile uses *like* or *as.*"

"How about an example, Amanda?"

I don't care for all this attention. There is a row of windows and the weather outside is sunny, but the skeletal trees have marked a transition between fall and winter. A pile of leaves rise in a death spiral from a gust of wind. It feels as if all eyes in the room are glued to me. "Sometimes we students are like trapped leaves, waiting for the winds of change."

"Exceptional and poetic, Amanda. That is what we call an indirect comparison, class."

Mrs. Brooks starts writing on the chalkboard again, when Mr. Appleton, the principal, appears at the classroom door. At first he is a shadow, until he opens the door a crack and motions for Mrs. Brooks. She goes to him and from behind the closed door they speak, just above a whisper. Without warning the door opens. They look directly at me.

My heart races into my throat, and I have to swallow the lump. Mrs. Brooks walks toward me.

"Amanda," she says, and she takes her glasses off and rubs her swollen eyes. "We need to see you in the hall for a minute."

I feel punched in the gut. I know this can't be a good thing. I'm hardly ever in trouble. Now, I feel eyes boring into the back of my head as she tells me, "You need to get your books too."

My heart is racing out of control, so I clutch my chest. Stumbling past uneven rows of desks, tripping over feet, I wonder if I shouldn't try climbing my way to the door, but I get there.

Mr. Appleton is perspiring. I'm lost in his dark wet eyes and then blinded by the reflection of light from his bald forehead. They both escort me across the hall into an empty science lab, a cold room with black marble counters and shiny sink faucets.

They tell me my mother is coming to get me, but they can't tell me why. She will tell me. I can sit on a stool and rest my head on the counter. I see a warped reflection of myself from the silver spigot, one of panic. As I look at them in the hallway speaking in hushed tones, I feel a sense of dread. Whirlwinds of dark similes and metaphors dance in my head.

But I am not alone for long…I pray until God's love fills my soul.

As I open my eyes, my mother fills the doorway wearing a white blouse and denim skirt. A vanilla sweater is draped over her shoulders as she extends her arms to me. Her hair looks angelic and silver as the light from the hall-way beams down on her.

In this moment, there is no place beside the light of heaven that I would rather run to.

I melt into her waiting arms but still do not know what all the fuss is about. Her eyes are moist but shimmering with hope. She holds me for a while, her chin resting on my hair. Then she crouches down and talks softly, where I can see her.

"I'm so sorry, sweetheart. Your father passed away."

She holds me by the shoulders, but I break free and go to the windows, wishing I could escape.

She follows. This time I let her hold me. She consumes me in her warmth. I'm not afraid. I'm not wondering where he is. "I never had a chance to pray away the danger. I never said good-bye."

She strokes my hair. "I know, honey. It doesn't seem right."

The hiccups start, and the sniffling that I can't control, but her love is so warm that it feels like God's fire building a wedge against the cold world.

"Not to worry," she says. "He and Annie will welcome us in heaven, and there will be no good-byes."

With tears blurring my vision, I look into my mother's eyes, filled with wonder. She does not blink or waver.

Together we steady each other as we walk down the long wide marble hall.

Suddenly, as if stabbed in the heart, I realize that Charity is nowhere in sight. "Charity," I say. "Does she know?"

My mother cups my face with her slender hands. "Yes, she knows."

As I whirl around, there she is, walking toward us holding a couple of fat textbooks, shouldering a backpack. She walks with purpose. Her thick locks of auburn hair dance and gleam in the penetrating sunlight as she approaches us near the entrance.

The three of us embrace. We huddle for a moment by the main door. I feel as if I have cried a faucet of tears. We part through the doors into a deceptively cold sun, toward my mother's car.

I look back to see the large white columns that give our school a fearsome look, like pictures in a book I've seen of the Roman coliseum. Hard to imagine it is the biggest building in our town. The large clock above the front pillars is what gets my attention. It is broken, its hands frozen in time. *Where has all the time gone? My father is gone.*

I dip inside the car and ride in the backseat with my aunt Charity, but for me she is the sister I never met. I can't imagine life without her.

My father once said, "Sometimes God takes us through faith where we may not ordinarily be willing to go if we had our hands on the wheel."

Mother drives with a firm grip; there is a strong resolve about her these days. She looks at us through the rearview mirror, and I suppose we seem to her in a trance. But I can't help notice her glassy eyes, resolve swimming inside of her. She says, "Your father had a big heart, and it just got to be too big for this world."

I fall asleep in my room on the day of funeral, dressed in a black skirt that comes to my knees. The black wool sweater insulates me. I feel as if spun into a cocoon.

In my dream, I see my father stepping softly over a crystal lake. He doesn't sink as he arrives at the silver shore. But it is not me he reaches for. He reaches for Annie, and I watch as Annie turns to me with a knowing smile. Somehow, I know that she is still a child, a bright child, and a child of hope. As I slip away from them, I hear a knock at my door.

"We'll wait for you downstairs," I hear Charity say. Shaking off the chills of my nap, I swipe a solitary tear of joy from my face. I run my fingers across the ridges and ruffles of the patchwork quilt my mother made for me when I was little.

I recall vividly the night I sat at her feet watching her work on it. After all, it was my special blanket. I said, "It looks kind of ugly on this side." My mother answered, "You must remember that above, and from heaven, the God who knows the end from the beginning knows the perfect order and how the lines and colors have a design, a pattern, and a purpose. We only see the ugly side, the ruined parts, the frayed and broken, seemingly imperfect lines, until one day the blanket is turned, and we stand in awe of his creation."

Somehow she must have known those words would carry me when I struggled to walk forward in this world, in such a day as this.

Throngs of people fill our church, and cars have lined the circle of the park near the gazebo until they choke Main Street. This makes my mother smile as we step into the church where my father faithfully served.

He had the heart attack in his office. A deacon found him, arms stretched out over his old oak desk as if he were tracing the carved initials of his children.

Before the service ends, I watch as my brother's lovely wife, Hailey, stands up to sing my father's favorite hymn. Her thick dark hair shines beneath the lights, and her smile infects us all with joy.

In shady green pastures, so rich and so sweet
God leads his dear children along;
Where the water's cool blow bathes the weary one's feet,
God leads his dear children along.

The congregation begins to sing with her on the chorus.

Some through the water, some through the flood,
Some through the fire, but all through the blood,
Some through great trials, but God gives a song
In the night season and all the day long.

Mother, Robert, Charity, and I, we all sit together in the front row. We bravely smile through tears while holding hands.

The service ends, and the "Paul Bears," as I like to call them, carry my father's casket down the steps into the hearse for the very short drive to the cemetery. Uncle Whitey with his Einstein hair leads the fleet. They securely wrap their fat hands around the golden handles, and we follow in confidence.

As we're leaving, I look out to see old Sheriff Brower getting into his police vehicle to lead the way to the gravesite. His hair is gray, and the sun has made his face rustic and worn. Mom says, "He will retire soon," and mentions that he has been reelected a record five times as the county sheriff.

My mother taps my shoulder and says, "Look, it's Skye Taylor." She points across the gazebo, where I see a young woman walk across the grass with a pair of stair-step boys following along in their shiny suits. "Amanda, she's the one you never met, the one who walked across a thin sheet of ice years ago and was rescued. They still call it the Miracle on Snowbird Lake."

Waves of people surround us while we stand over my father's grave. A sense of cover and comfort grows around us, to know that he touched so many other lives, a sea of people stretching out along the withered grass.

As we say a prayer and our last good-bye this side of heaven, I'm reminded of what my father once said, when as a child I held his hand while others wept for a loved one. He whispered in my ear, "We offer a prayer today, not for the one who has passed, but for the living loved ones who must finish life's journey of faith without them."

We all hold our roses until the moment when we hear the clank of shovels and watch the dirt scatter on the mahogany casket.

As the crowd thins and cars pull away, we start our long walk beside the emerald-green strip along the rutted gravel path. We watch, curiously, as a car pulls along the edge of the road. A young girl with dark hair who looks to be in her late teens steps out with a yellow rose. There is a young man, perhaps her husband, waiting in the driver's seat. A child is strapped into a car seat in the rear. With a determined smile, she dashes toward us, running in her bare feet, holding her dress to her knees.

My mother looks up with a puzzled expression across her face. "I wonder who this is."

Charity and I look at each other and shrug our shoulders.

Rob and Hailey stand close to my mother with a look of wonder.

As she gets close enough to talk, she has to catch her breath. She has diamond-blue eyes, and she looks at me first.

"I hope I'm not too late to pay my respects."

My mother cups her face in astonishment. "Why…why you're the little girl in the wheelchair!"

She hugs my mother and says, "I'm Miranda."

"I knew it," Mother answers, and she can't hold back the tears that trail like rivulets on her weathered face.

"I made a promise," Miranda says, and she walks over to where my father is in the ground, placing her rose in the falling dirt. "I will never forget you."

She walks over to where Charity and I are standing, and she hugs me. "Are you the baby I saw in the hospital that day? Are you Amanda?"

"Yes." I nod.

She gives me a note scrunched in her hand. As I unfurl it, she gives Charity and the rest of my family good-bye hugs. Then she leaves, sprinting toward her family.

The day of the fire I thought for sure I would die. All was black, but then suddenly this angel appeared. He covered me in wings of blue and we flew through a window. Your father saved my life that day, and I hope to live a life that is worth saving.

The bottom of the note reads, *I don't know if it's in the Bible or not, but I've heard, "Love is not just something you say, it's something you do."*

As I watch her driving away with her family, I think about something else my father used to tell us. "The recipe for a good life is to have a pinch of faith, but be sure you add a heaping spoon of love, because if you don't, your life won't rise to the place it deserves to be."

A wind lifts from the hills and skirts through fallen leaves as I take Charity's hand and we walk the well-worn path before us.

And now abideth faith, hope, charity, these three; but
the greatest of these is charity.

1 CORINTHIANS 13:13

Acknowledgments

First, I would like to mention Jan Ackerson, who taught me the value of a good editor. Without her professional ability and keen perception of the written word, I may not have been brave enough to offer this story to the public.

Second, I would like to thank my dear friend Ingrid from Canada, whose pen name, *Spiritual Echo*, speaks for itself. She championed this story like no other and all but guaranteed that if I entered it into a contest it would be the winner. Thanks for being the catalyst I needed, never offering me pity during times of self-loathing, but only hope.